I have explored this planet *Homo sapiens* calls Earth: all of the nations, states, and provinces that they have arbitrarily carved on its surface, at the expense of uncountable lives. I explored the planet's fields and all its oceans. I roamed the streets, the cities and the structures. I studied the laws, rules, principles, and philosophies. I saw all I had to see, and I talked to as many of their kind as I could, in an effort to better understand them.

And my visit is about to conclude.

When this book is published, it means I will have left this planet. I will not be missed, because no one will remember me... I have never *personally* told anyone who I really am, and I don't plan on ever changing that.

Once I'm gone, however, I will be free to publish this story.

No one will believe it anyway.

1

Henry Lindell

Autobiography of an Extraterrestrial

AUTOBIOGRAPHY OF AN EXTRATERRESTRIAL

A Henry Lindell Book

ISBN 978-0-9905429-8-8

CONTENTS

PREFACE

"Excuse me... what time do you have?"

She was startled by my question. Perfectly innocent, of course, but I had caught her off guard. She was swaying in unison with the rest of the passengers as the subway cars stubbornly tried to grab hold of the line's sinuous tracks. A more observant person might have noticed that I hardly moved at all, another of the many distinguishing marks that screams my un-*Homo sapiens* nature and origin, but nowadays, people hardly bother to observe anymore. At least long enough to notice such details.

"Oh... let me check." She reached for her phone, and noticed it was missing. The blood drained from her face almost immediately.

"Is something wrong?" I asked her, trying to sound sincerely unaware of why her expression had deteriorated so suddenly, managing a decent rendition of surprise.

"My phone... it's missing!" She looked down, scanning the floor, trying, hoping, to see it.

I looked at the young subway rider standing a few feet away from her. He was looking out the window, listening to music with his earphones, avoiding us, clearly. Purposefully. I could sense that he wanted to get off the train as soon as possible, although he was trying very hard to appear calm and oblivious to these developments.

"What color is your phone?" I asked her, even though I already knew the answer to the question.

"Silver with white. Why... did you see it?" I instantly became her prime suspect. She stared back at me with a mixture of fear and aggressiveness, ready to confront me, perhaps. But she also had a glimmer of hope, her optimistic nature stubbornly showing its face. I stored that quantum moment for later use.

I lowered my voice, down to practically a whisper, and slowly leaned towards her, making sure to keep my arms behind my body as a sign of respect. "Yes. I know who has it. Relax; I can help you get it back."

I had seen these little nuances occur hundreds—no, thousands of times—during my stays here on Earth, all exaggerations aside. At first, I had always—immediately!—intervened, confronting the offenders directly, startling them. No law against that kind of interference. But this didn't always end well for all parties involved, in one way or another. Now, at times, I choose to simply let these things happen, to ignore them. But playing the oblivious bystander doesn't generally do it for me, I must admit. So more often than not, especially so close to my possible date of a departure, I do get involved. The feeling of helping those in need is unique, the processing potential truly realized.

"Excuse me, what time do you have?" I asked the guilty individual this time, pointing at an imaginary watch on my wrist to aid me in my attempt to get through to him, taking note of the fact that the music blasting in his ears rendered him completely deaf to the world around him.

He was not happy with the interruption. I guess that more out of habit than anything else, he removed one of his earphones. "What did you say?" he asked.

"Do *you* have the time?" Emphasis on the word *you* to humor his narcissistic side.

"No." It was barely audible, rude, and as he said this, he raised his upper lip and shook his head, clearly trying too much to make it clear that he was bothered by my untimely and unwarranted interruption. He started to put his earphone back in his ear, *subtly* letting me know that he was effectively ending the conversation. I immediately stopped his motion with my hand, using just enough force to intimidate him.

"Actually, you do have the time. Well, not exactly on a wristwatch. Like my imaginary one here. But something else that does tell time. If you know where to look for it…"

The young man was now very uncomfortable, nervous. He knew he had been caught stealing the phone from the clueless subway rider. I could see him desperately trying to wriggle himself somehow out of this one, pondering his options. He probably thought I was one of those undercover police officers that are supposed to roam the subways precisely to stop crimes such as the one he had committed, at least as far as his fictitious view of reality would have him believed, based on what I assumed to be his massive TV knowledge.

I evaluated the quantum histories that were feasible given the present set of circumstances, and opted for the one that would probably end as positive as possible for both of the beings involved in this minuscule–albeit very personal–drama that was unfolding. We are all, after all, computational structures that can process novel and positive algorithms if given adequate nudges during development. I always try to help out, whenever possible. No one structure is computationally worthless. Not a single one.

I turned to look at her. "As I was saying ma'am, we are trying to educate users of our wonderful public transportation system, users like you, how to safeguard their belongings at all times. Now take your cellphone, for example. You did not notice it was missing until I asked you what time it was…" I raised my voice, drawing the attention of the other riders, on purpose. Not because I bask in the limelight, but because it was part of my chosen storyline.

9

"My partner here, Jack, he *borrowed* it. And you didn't feel a thing! We only did this to prove a point, but this could have happened to you for real." I smiled as I said this, putting on a show.

She realized what I was doing. And so did the young man. All three of us knew what had really transpired, but we all played our part, pretending that we didn't know what was really happening. It *saved face* all around, as *Homo sapiens* like to say, although no one was fooling anyone here. Even the other passengers could sense that something was not quite right, though of course, they did not interfere. Regardless, as I quickly realized after my first studies of *Homo sapiens* behavior, this is not an uncommon state of affairs–pretending, playing along, fooling the self–although unfortunately, neither is the victimizing of fellow *Homo sapiens* beings in any of its multiple modalities. Not surprisingly, I have found *Homo sapiens* to be extremely creative in executing often complex activities of the latter kind. And quite illogical and perplexing in their (innate?) behavioral characteristics such as the former, as well.

I turned around to face the young man once more. "You win again, Jack! I thought she was going to notice, but I was wrong. You are a perfect ten for ten today. That is truly impressive!" I slapped him on the shoulder playfully, with the familiarity that two co-workers that spend their days together for hours on end would possess, while I swiftly removed the silver and white cell phone from his front coat pocket during the *amicable* exchange. I truly enjoyed the moment, I must confess.

"Here you go," I told her as I handed the phone back to her. Raising my voice, I concluded the impromptu show with a final word to the wise: "Remember to always keep your belongings close to you, and your valuables, such as your cell phone, wallet, jewelry, and loved-ones, within your line of sight, at all times!"

As if on cue, one of the many voices that all seem somehow so familiar to the millions of regular New York subway riders, that of the subway conductor, announced our current state of affairs over the PA system. "This is the Manhattan bound 'Q' train. The next stop is 34 Street-Herald Square. Please stand clear of the doors." Metallic, and surprisingly clear and understandable, unlike most such PA systems found everywhere on Earth.

The train started to slow down, stubbornly screeching as it always does, especially when taking on a curve. Metal against metal has a tendency to behave this way. Humbleness aside, *Homo sapiens* technology can be very quaint, compared to what I know and even personally possess, and to what I have seen elsewhere in this and in other universes. And yet I find it strangely fascinating and unique, captivating even—or maybe the expression that I'm really looking for here is naive? Well, to be fair, all civilizations clumsily bump their way in the dark, slowly progressing towards the light of cosmic computational enlightenment. *Rome was not built in a day...*

"Well, Jack, this is our stop. Let's go... we have other subway riders to educate!"

I turned around to face her one last time. "And thank you for your time... for letting us provide a bit of sound advice to you and to your fellow subway riders." I winked once, smiling. She understood perfectly well what had happened, and simply returned the smile. She felt slightly ashamed, slightly hurt, but at the same time relieved that her cellphone was once again in her possession. She was too dumbstruck to actually vocalize anything, so she ended the exchange with a slight nod. Enough *said*.

When the train came to a full stop and the doors opened, I grabbed the young man by the elbow and escorted him out. I really didn't have to exert much force to get him moving. I figured he would try to run as soon as we were on the platform, but I held him tightly, grabbing his backpack with my other hand just to be safe. I was not done with him just yet. Act two was just about to begin.

After the doors closed behind us and the train sped away, leaving both of us alone, surrounded by the station's multiple narrow, riveted metal columns, I looked into his eyes and asked him again: "Do you have the time?"

He laughed. Not out of joy, but rather, I could see, out of amusement, amazement, stupefaction.

"What do you want, man? What the heck?" he asked angry, afraid.

I smiled. "*Your* time!"

"Are you on drugs, man? You better let me go or I'm calling the cops… Right now!" He looked desperately for someone–anyone –that might be joining us on the platform. He felt scared, his adrenaline beginning to be a factor, his body temperature oddly dropping, but his heart rate dutifully accelerating. There was no one around.

"Quantum fluctuation readings indicate that you do have time." I couldn't really elaborate. Being *Homo sapiens*, he completely misunderstands this meta-universal concept.

In his neuronal network, I could make out two rapidly deteriorating branchings. There weren't that many, fortunately for him, fortunately for this planet, fortunately for this *Homo sapiens* species, and well, ultimately, for the meta-universe given the fact that we are all in this together. I operated quickly, configuring my morphing unit as a quantum sensor and an electromagnetic wave generator, which I happened to be carrying with me today, guiding the high energy particles, finding the points where the synapses needed to be removed, and where new branches needed to be created. Some brains couldn't be dealt with this way, requiring nothing short of metabolic and genetic modifications instead, in addition to a procedure such as this one. Had that been the case, I would've had to let him go. There are simply too many *Homo sapiens* on the planet that fall under that second category for me to be able to do anything about it. My mission here would never come to an end.

I was careful to leave this experience intact after determining that it would be necessary for him to be perfectly aware that this had been a turning point in his life; his central nervous system (well, his brain–for the most part) would be able to draw computational strength from this experience whenever that need arose.

After I was finished—the procedure took only 8.1 seconds to complete—his anger and discomfort evaporated. He took out his own cell phone, pressed a button to wake it up, looked at the home screen, and said, "You wanted to know the time... it's 3:47 p.m." The words were a bit slurred, maybe not noticeably so to most—if not all—*Homo sapiens*; but certainly detectable by me.

"Thank you," I replied, releasing him. He was stable now, almost normal.

He walked away slowly, shaking his head. He somehow felt the truth of what happened on that platform, but he was unable to actually *process* it, to hold it in his consciousness long enough to make sense of it, as is often the case with these interventions. In the days to come the memory of the event would be sharper, clearer, with a lot more detail. It would turn concrete, and yet remain always elusive. A mental itch that he could never be able to scratch, and yet it would help his computational processes remain grounded.

As he rode the escalator that led to the street up above, he turned around, wondering what had happened to him, expecting an additional sign from me, anything that would help him make sense of these events. But he was no longer of my concern; I was already engaged in something else—sending information to Pris through the metanet, actually—while I waited for the next train to arrive. Having prematurely bailed out of the last one, not having yet reached my destination, I needed to get back on the Q line, Manhattan bound, once again.

I was headed a couple of stations beyond this one... and I didn't have much time to spare. Pressing matters to attend to.

1. Origins

Homo sapiens would have a hard time understanding that I am *a collection*–rather than a single unit–very unlike how all members of their species are today, I wish to make that perfectly clear from the start. And this difficulty does not stem from my constant apparent-contradictory use of the English pronoun '*I*', but is rather a direct consequence of the *Homo sapiens'* species particular neuronal wiring, of their current location within the evolutionary path they have inadvertently (so far, at least) embarked on.

It should also be understood from the very beginning that every time I am here on Earth, whenever I desire to transmit my ideas, experiences, and perceptions, I am forced to try to convey my alien reality using the many different tongues (or languages, whatever you prefer) that may happen to be in use at the time of my visit by *Homo sapiens*, obviously a commonly impossible task! Using any of the communication *systems* that I have access to would be futile since *Homo sapiens* beings are not capable of handling them given their current evolutionary stage. And these systems cannot really be taught, either. *Homo sapiens* lacks not only the neuronal wiring but also the peripherals that could open up that door.

All *Homo sapiens* beings communicate using a system of words that are not surprisingly ill-suited to the experiences beyond those that *Homo sapiens* have encountered in their two hundred thousand years or so of existence as full-fledged *Homo sapiens*. But rightly so, of course; after all, how can a civilization be expected to come up with words for concepts that they have never experienced? And how can they be expected to conceptualize experiences that they lack the sensors for? Ergo my reality and that of others like me, regardless of our specific origins, evolutionary paths, or physical locations, are beyond the current *Homo sapiens* experience, and not subject to be described using any of the *Homo sapiens* written or verbal communication systems; not even their mental wirings are adequately suited to comprehend my reality. At least not clearly, perfectly, without having to conjure up images using ill-suited words, an art in its own right, but a technique that is inherently prone to being completely misunderstood.

And yet this is an autobiography (well, an incomplete one at that, to be precise), written in a *Homo sapiens* language–*primarily English*–, for *Homo sapiens* to read, interpret, comprehend, and process. Not an easy task, nor one that is guaranteed to happen... Some–let me be blunt, at the price of appearing pedantic–*most*! of my experiences, realities, and possibilities, will thus remain outside of what can be grasped by the *Homo sapiens* mind. And it is not even my choice, since I cannot force ideas and experiences into a being's brain. But what is relevant to this twenty-first century species, as far as I am concerned –well, actually, as far as *we* are concerned, since *here* that pronoun should be used–will be included in these writings. Relevant, of course, only if we assume that all goes according to plan, for the universe is full of quantum fluctuations that eventually crystalize, defining the reality that is experienced by macroscopic sentient beings such as ourselves.

And so I'll begin.

On this occasion, I set foot here on Earth 2190 days, four hours and 3.12 minutes ago (UTC-5[1])–excuse my precision–relative to

---

[1] UTC: Coordinated Universal Time.

the instant in which I write this, by the way, at which point I immediately deployed myself throughout this planetary orbiting mass, third in succession from the star locally referred to as the Sun. All this time, I have been practically *simultaneously!* experiencing all aspects of planet Earth, from its geography to its biodiversity to the vastness of the *Homo sapiens* condition.

But I will keep this linear and subjectively separated in bits and pieces, in tune with how the typical *Homo sapiens* brain envisions and perceives its reality. Parallel processing and conscientious quantum thought is a process that takes tens of millions of years[2] to develop, billions of years even in some extreme and well documented cases, and even then, only after a minimal intelligence threshold is crossed (something *Homo sapiens* achieved as a species a mere forty thousand years ago).

My collection of different quantum realities, superimposed, waves of probability states that have collapsed simultaneously in different locations–as all quantum matters eventually are–can be clumsily, stubbornly, presented linearly and in chunks (though not without loss of information). But bear in mind that I am a collection of different selves, each unique, and yet all *simultaneously* the same. We collectively experience and process existence, wherever and whenever we may have access to localized data, and certainly not in a linear way!

It will make everything easier if I assign myself a name. Although I use many during my earthly travels, for the purposes of this autobiographyI will use the surname of Roy (the name *Henry Lindell* is a technicality that I need not get into). As for my only team member–a purposefully-built being, if you will–I will use the name Pris. To the *Homo sapiens* naked eye, our internal structures–other than those that are normally found between the male and female members of the species–are indistinguishable from each other (FYI: externally, I have taken the form of a *Homo sapiens* male, and Pris of a *Homo sapiens* female).

---

[2] Except when otherwise specified, time units used refer to those defined by *Homo sapiens* on Earth.

In fact, even if we were both scanned side by side using any of the methods available to the twenty-first century *Homo sapiens* civilization, we would appear to be of identical physiological composition, *Homo sapiens* even, at least on the surface of things (for only an atomic-level scan could provide clues of our extraterrestrial origin). That's because our respective differences run deeper than that; they could truly only be uncovered in our origin, by accessing and analyzing and comparing our Primary Selves, our sources of being, which reside somewhere in the meta-universe, in the metanet, reachable only through the singularity. Of course, we do have unique processing structures that are incorporated almost unobtrusively within the *Homo sapiens* structure, which gives us sensory and computational abilities that are clearly of extraterrestrial origin.

I was immediately struck by how long I'd been away. If not so much on a meta-universe time scale (*ha!*), certainly so in terms of the progress achieved by the *Homo sapiens* civilization since I had last been here... On that occasion, I had departed in the year 1453 of Earth's Common Era (CE).

I am forced to conclude that the progress achieved has been noticeable (though not evenly so in all matters important to the species slash civilization slash ecosystems slash Earth, and not equally amongst all individuals−or groups of individuals−of the *Homo sapiens* species itself). This species does seem particularly keen in perpetuating socio-economic injustice, denying their most vulnerable the most basic of needs, while the few opulently and grossly swim in superfluous riches. Historic and environmental factors clearly deter some *Homo sapiens* groups from independently reaching a healthy condition, and it does not help the more vulnerable *whatsoever* that some even profit while the true potential of the under-developed remains mutilated by factors outside of the control of the underdeveloped themselves, or by true inaction of those in power, the *over-privileged,* where it really matters, such as in adequate nutrition, or in the education of the young.

Archaic economic models, instinctively if not consciously supported by the *Homo sapiens*' elite few, serve only to perpetuate the existing grotesquely-comical socioeconomic conditions. I must say (without judgement, since I am judgement-free) that as an outsider it is painful to watch. Change couldn't come fast enough in this regard. The computational waste makes the meta-universe weep, to paint an image that *Homo sapiens* may understand.

Allow my processing structures to utter a sigh.

Moving on…

Whenever I am on this planet, I interact with as many *Homo sapiens* as possible, although I keep my true nature to myself *−not a matter of choice, but rather of law*. Among those I have met that stand out for reasons that will become clear later on is Deborah−I always liked that name, and it somehow fits, in a twisted way. Note that it is not an actual name, of course. Nor that of any other person that I mention here; just one more technicality that I will adhere to, in order to keep all parties sufficiently safe from identification.

"May I help you with those bags?" I had asked her. It was early evening, twilight settling in, the sky a deep, dark blue−as perceived by the typical *Homo sapiens* eye. There was a light drizzle, nothing to really run away from, and given the fact that the temperature was just below seventy-six degrees Fahrenheit, actually very enjoyable to members of the *Homo sapiens* species.

She was on the sidewalk, walking along a bit distractedly, and had just inadvertently bumped into me while I performed some calculations, exploring a set of quantum matrices that required my attention. A few items fell out from her bags, which I promptly picked up and handed back to her.

"Oh… I'm sorry!" She had said as she nervously laughed.

"Nothing to be sorry about. I'm just glad nothing broke."

"Are you referring to your leg, or to my items?" Her smile had seemed warm and real.

I delayed a few seconds, basking in the quantum moment. "Strong guy like me? I am practically unbreakable... but let me help you... those bags look heavy. And it would be best if your purchases arrived to its intended destination, each in one piece as their manufacturers, I assume, intended."

"Well, why not. I am tired of carrying them, and I am not going very far." She was lowering her guard, perceiving that I was trustworthy? I had quickly learned how to operate a smile, back when *Homo sapiens* first developed it as a way to positively interact with others.

We walked for a couple of blocks, talking about trivial matters. It was pleasing for me on many different levels. For her, I knew she was simply enjoying the *fluffiness* of the moment.

She stopped well short of her final destination. *A stranger was a stranger.* "Well, thank you for helping me. It was really nice." She was being sincere.

I finished the quantum scan I had begun moments earlier and confirmed that there was something worth exploring in greater detail. I couldn't be sure what it was... not with the rain coming down on us, a distorting curtain that stood between her body and my sensors, preventing me from performing a focused reading. The raindrops interfered with the quantum waves a lot more than the atmospheric components did, regardless of its typically moist nature. The cosmic-wide weirdness of the all-important molecule −two hydrogen atoms and one oxygen atom, chemically joined −is far-reaching.

"You never did tell me your name. I am Roy, by the way."

"*Peeeep*," she replied without hesitation. Assume she said *Deborah*. Her dark brown eyes glittered, enhanced by the water droplets that reflected the light coming from the street lamp next to us.

"Listen, I am new in the city... just got here last week, actually. Would you care to have coffee with me? There is a shop just around the corner, pretty decent stuff. My treat..."

She looked down at her feet, not knowing how to respond? I guess she was in a particularly open state of mind that particular day, because she ended up saying yes, agreeing to my impromptu invitation.

It was established that we were to meet two days later, on a Saturday, at eleven in the morning. If she couldn't make it, she would leave a message for me at the coffee shop. She was clearly not ready to trade phone numbers (or text messages) just yet.

I waved goodbye as I left half-hurriedly, knowing very well she wouldn't want me to notice that she was still a few blocks from her building. I wanted to spare her from the awkwardness of that revelation.

I went back to where I had originally been standing when the chance encounter took place (perfectly within the realm of the probabilistic, I computed), and continued to perform the calculations that I had been willing to interrupt.

It is hard to describe the process I was involved in, knowing the limitations of the *Homo sapiens* perception. But analogies can be powerful *bridgers* of concepts that are unfamiliar, no matter how unreachable they may be... which prompts me to give it a try: quantum sensors inside me interact with my computational structure (or rather, my equivalent of the *Homo sapiens* brain), and I am thus able to simultaneously sense these overlapping probabilities, collapsing relevant waves of uncertainty as need be while ignoring the unlikely relevant, and thus exploring trillions of possibilities at once. The process itself is almost involuntary, like when a *Homo sapiens* recalls a datum: somehow, the information is there, it can be sensed, not seen nor touched nor smelled, and yet it is there, palpable, within the realm of the accomplishable by the mind. Likewise, I perform calculations that are necessary to accomplish a goal−part of an algorithmic endeavor−, or simply to accommodate what *Homo sapiens* might call a *je ne sais quoi...* but that they know (or feel?) to be deterministic thoughts that have crystallized in this space-time. It is a process that is impossible to sum up using any combination of words from any twenty-first century *Homo sapiens* language, and yet it is the primary activity of beings like me.

****

I finished a few minutes later. I had been half sitting, half standing–leaning really–against a high ledge that guarded the side of the aging Manhattan building's facade. The sky was completely dark by now, and although *Homo sapiens* eyes couldn't perceive it, the stars shined for me–as bright as I allowed them to, simply by adjusting at will my electromagnetic sensors (temporarily overriding preset fuzzy-logic algorithms).

Somewhere up there, my ship waited patiently, along with my ship-bound self. It would be some time, perhaps, before it would leave this star system, on its way to other civilizations that required *our?* attention.

I went to the nearest restaurant and ordered something to eat. Although this was a very inefficient way of supplying my living tissues with the energy and the materials necessary for survival, I do tend to stick to the local customs, especially when immersed in a planet with a species that has a social and a cultural level of evolution as complex as that of the *Homo sapiens.*

As far as beings that are part of me are concerned, beings that are directly involved in this mission, they were out there somewhere, continuing to explore, to connect, helping people carry bags, or giving directions, or whatever else presented itself as an excuse to *engage*, as well as collecting DNA samples, performing brain scans, and collecting innumerable data from the planet and all of its inhabitants, regardless of its evolutionary state. But beyond that, they were involved in the never-ending process of simply *being, processing, computing.*

Me and my other selves–of which I am a part of, by the way, since what you would call *the original me* has long ceased to exist in its original, simpler, format, and is certainly not *Homo sapiens* in appearance *at all!*–would never reunite, for there is no need and no purpose to that, and therefore, not even part of the design. Our experiences, however, have merged, do merge, and will merge wherever my processing structures, linked, may happen to operate.

All in the pursuit of the goal.

2. Paris, France

While *I* was talking to Deborah, back in Manhattan, *I* was also in Paris, France. A physically different version of me, as is the case of all my *replicas*. None of us look anything alike. And why should we? Although one and the same, we do each occupy distinct space-time realms, which ultimately gives us a sense of individuality all the same.

Gustave was talking very fast, warning me about something.

"Roy, they are coming! Please, we have to get out of here!"

It was close to one in the morning, not too late considering the sleeping habits of the locals–something parisians are very well known for. It had started out as a *Thursday night* (technically speaking, now it was Friday, but that's not important).

"I hear you, Gustave. But you have not told me who is coming… the police? *Flics*?" I asked him quietly, trying to calm him down.

"No! I would have left already if that was the case!" He seemed very disturbed by the mere mention of the word (*flic*s is cops in French, for those not familiar with the language).

"Well then, who is coming?"

"The man I told you about from this morning, most likely with his entourage. I want to avoid a confrontation! Let's go!"

I was finished collecting the samples anyway, so I put my instruments away, pocketed the container, and signaled him that we could be on our way.

Truth be told, we were not even invading the grounds of the Montparnasse Cemetery. We were on Rue Victor Schoelcher, near the intersection with Rue Froidevaux. We had parked our car right next to the cemetery's wall (an oversized van to better shield us from prying eyes), on one of the individualized ad-hoc parking spaces that protrude from the street, or if you prefer, that are buried into the sidewalk, wedged between two trees. *Either or.* Taking genetic samples required my physical presence, and even though my instruments did all the work by themselves, a fleet of minute, insect-sized robots capable of sniffing the valuable specimens and storing them safely for later use, I still wanted to be there to coordinate their efforts; the whole process was faster and allowed for a level of fine-tuning that would otherwise not be possible.

Two cars were slowly approaching us, hence Gustave's concern; but as it turned out, they were a semi-lost tourist party looking for directions (the quintessential vacationers daring enough to rent a car in a foreign country). After sending them off in the right direction, assuming they could follow my instructions correctly, Gustave and I got on the van and headed towards the 16th arrondissement, near the Trocadéro, where I had secured a short-term rental, very minute in size but more than sufficient for my needs.

Gustave was quiet, more so than usual. I figured he had been stressed out by the imaginary arrival of the "morning man and his possible entourage", and was in the process of slowly eliminating all the adrenaline traveling through his arteries and veins. I left him alone, clueless as to what had scared him so much, but reluctant to ask him about it, figuring it might upset him.

He dropped me off and quickly sped away, barely saying goodbye.

"Au revoir!" I yelled to him as he fled, with his demons in tow.

I went up to my apartment, a very expensive and tastefully decorated one bedroom flat, and immediately began to process the samples, pausing only to turn on the TV, not caring what channel I had last left it on–I could extract that particular datum, but purposefully chose not to.

Since it had been hundreds of years since I had last been on Earth, this was the only way to document the genetic variations of the outstanding, regardless of their supra-*Homo sapiens* activity or activities of choice. It would be ideal if I could examine their brains physically, but that, of course, is usually impossible. Their organs can hardly be expected to survive the burial practices of the seventeenth, eighteenth, nineteenth, or twentieth centuries. And unfortunately, I could not leave any ad-hoc scanners behind, since there exists the very real danger that they may be found. Alien technology... a definite no-no if I am going to keep The Process clean and within the guidelines of what is appropriate, given the Earth's current evolutionary stage. Surveillance ants, moths, spiders, and the like, do keep tabs on numerous issues that are deemed vital to monitor, but anything beyond that had not been deployed, nor would that change in the future as long as *Homo sapiens* roamed this planet.

And so genes must do, although even these may be damaged to the point of being worthless. I was hoping that all twenty-three pairs of chromosomes of a specific few were intact, no matter how improbable this seemed (Henri Poincaré, Jean-Paul Sartre, Porfirio Díaz, and Carlos Fuentes, to name but a few of those I was particularly craving for from this particular burial site, Montparnasse).

The task is quite straightforward, certainly comprehensible to the average twenty-first century scientifically-knowledgeable *Homo sapiens* being. After scanning the samples from each *specimen*, the genetic sequence can be digitally established. Sometimes, it is necessary to take chunks of DNA from one cell sample in order to complement the data gathered from another one (the latter usually being the most uncompromised specimen, conveniently labeled the master-cell); at other times, whole chromosomes need to be replaced, or recreated from multiple cell sources (all from the same individual, of course!). If there is a section that is damaged in every one of the individual's available cell samples, I may use statistically-derived replacements to fill the gap, but only if the missing section is deemed inconsequential for the purpose of the study (in this case, brain functionality). However, as an inherently chaotic system, the results would quickly become dubious at best, completely unreliable at worst.

Once the digitalized DNA data transfer is complete, a quantum-level simulator creates a virtual replica of the individual. During this process, nothing physical is actually created, but this difference is truly insignificant. The DNA is given a virtual cellular home, in fact transformed into a zygote, and is placed in a virtual womb, together with the nutrients that were typically present at the time of conception given the socioeconomic and geographic conditions of the original event. Although not a perfect process, since most of these systems are computationally irreducible, the results are typically very revealing.

From that moment on, the virtual development proceeds exactly as it would in the real, physical world. Physics and chemistry laws are precisely known, and so the simulator is able to recreate all aspects of zygote evolution: from one cell to the near trillion of cells that a *Homo sapiens* baby typically possess at birth. During the simulation process, environmental factors are considered, as close as possible to those found in the individual's original surroundings, all guided by the delicate interplay of genes and their environment. And it only takes a few minutes to quantumly compute this evolution.

This process cannot be bypassed by any means whatsoever: although some systems can be simplified (modeled) to the point where knowing the value of certain key variables can be used to compute a desired result (or to pinpoint certain desired characteristics of the system under study), DNA and its multiple by-products do not normally lend themselves to this type of mathematical (including statistical-biological) modeling, especially when one is interested in observing whole systems and system interactions, as opposed to individual, discrete-valued components such as eye color, for example.

Cellular automata (which *Homo sapiens* has only begun to discover and explore, spearheaded by Stephen Wolfram barely thirty years ago, having only scratched its vast potential), more accurately resembles the appropriate type of task that is required.

Homo sapiens brains, of course, are influenced by more than the applicable genes and/or the environment experienced inside the womb. Impossible to replicate with any relevant degree of certainty, I stop at what would have been the moment of birth. And although much of the brain's development occurs later on in the life of the *Homo sapiens* individual, and in fact never stops until death, a lot of the *Homo sapiens* potential can be determined in the 38 week old brain. Key intelligence and personality traits are already established (in potential, if not *ipso facto*), a product of the particular DNA code of the individual, the chemicals it produces and regulates, and the chemical gradients that bathe both the inside and the outside of every cell in the body.

I could let the simulator continue on to later stages in the evolution of the individual, feeding it statistically-relevant life experiences, allowing the virtual person to define itself into adulthood. However, this would only provide a glimpse of one on the infinitely many possible versions of the same person, not the one that actually *occurred*.

I do sometimes generate adult versions just to see the effect that different environments would've had on the particular individual being studied, even though these virtual entities never turn out to closely resemble the real, historical, actual being that physically roamed the Earth. But I do create these versions anyway, and keep some of them computationally active, in the virtual world that harbors them, so that I may continue to study them, interact with them, and ultimately, enjoy their individual processing potential. A virtual version of myself is permanently active inside

29

that virtual world (there are actually many different virtual versions of myself at any given moment), one more of the many dimensions that I simultaneously operate on. That virtual reality is quite enjoyable and revealing of the laws that govern complex, chaotic systems. It is just as real as reality itself. A sets within the set of the cosmos...

In some cases, I let several versions of the same person inhabit a particular *ecosystem*, coexisting with other versions of itself, without really knowing they are *clones* of each other. For example, Aristotle has seven clones on a particular virtual set, and he is not alone in that regard: so does Hilbert, the mathematician. Physical resemblances are dealt with by tweaking facial features, minutely so (enough to throw each individual off the scent, but not so much so that it deviates dramatically from the physical versions), while one remains unchanged. Randomness gets to choose. Often, virtual barriers are erected between virtual worlds, creating islands within, either to maintain historical integrity or simply because the algorithm that I happen to be using warrants it. It is, of course, mostly an intellectual exercise. Never meant to be an emulator of the history of Earth, since that is inherently impossible.

As of date, the universe that Earth inhabits has proved to be statistically within the norm as far as the quality and quantity of intelligent beings produced and currently in existence is concerned. And there is only so much that is done in order to help this process along. But Earth has definitely shown the most promise—so far. Nothing really special, mind you, so the arrogance may be dispensed with; after all, some planet must ultimately possess that distinction on any given region of space-time, of a universe, of the cosmos. On the other hand, there were a few interesting civilizations that sprang up on second generation star systems (first generation stars simply lacked the abundance of heavier elements necessary for intelligence structures to *naturally* evolve, so they could never really compete), but unfortunately the planets and satellites in which they evolved were typically too close to the galactic core and thus were not able to survive the catastrophic events that are so common in those regions of space.

On an unrelated note, it was ultimately one of these civilizations, their specific species, that did not survive, for their genetic influence still lives on. *Wink-wink*.

After analyzing all nine-hundred and four individuals (read *persons*, not cell samples, for I had tens of millions of the latter), eight-hundred and ninety-nine of them were viable, and were thus virtually developed to their thirty-eight week old developmental stage. As it turned out, the samples of all of the historical figures that were on my wish-list had been good enough to be viable, save for one. Not a bad outcome at all. They would be inhabiting virtual worlds after a brief quarantine cycle.

Shortly after completing this first stage of the analysis, I noticed something that alarmed me. Most of the virtual beings possessed a unique chemical gradient that permeated the hippocampus and prefrontal cortex, clearly key genes at play. I quantumly-computed variants of these specimens in order to determine the genes that were responsible for this unexpected chemical behavior. Up to my last visit, this had never been seen.

In essence, quantum matrices allow to quickly explore which DNA changes would eliminate the chemical gradient I had detected; without the power of multiple (simultaneous) quantum states, this process would simply be too impractical (it would take millions of years to check, due to the multi-leveled interplay that individual genes display). Quantum analysis allows exponential parallel processing (using superposition and state entanglement), which dramatically reduces computation time, compared to linear (classical) processing systems. *Homo sapiens* has–not surprisingly–already begun to explore this powerful far-reaching process…

A few seconds later, I had my answer. All of the individuals that had the enhanced chemical gradient had the same five key gene mutations (the paragraphs of these five genes were strewn about in different chromosomes, and had thus remained undetected to the nascent *Homo sapiens* genetic researcher, although for how much longer, it would be impossible to guess). Obviously, this could not be statistically explained by the random mutations that do take place in the course of evolution. An outside force was responsible for this, no question about it, which had to be exogenous to Earth. In a few days, I would have a lot more data to support the conclusion I had already arrived to: from additional virtual nine-month old virtual *Homo sapiens*, from the DNA sourced from other geographical places on Earth, and from the samples being collected from *Homo sapiens* that are alive today.

The theory that I already had in *mind* was not a pleasant one. At all.

3. Boston, MA

No matter where on Earth I happened to take the DNA samples from, once I developed those that were viable, specifically those that belonged to *Homo sapiens* beings that had been born after 1455 CE and that had led outstanding lives in one way or another (either through their craft, or because of their socio-economic influence), the Montparnasse results were replicated. All these *positives* had a particular set of genes in common that no other *Homo sapiens* possessed: genetic variations that would be impossible to be present in such a large number of people purely by coincidence (read *by chance mutations or environmental factors*).

And so it was obvious. Someone with an agenda had artificially mutated specific individuals sometime after I had left Earth the last time I had been here. Not what I would expect to find at all.

I could only assume that many more people had been DNA-altered, but for some reason or another, had not successfully bloomed (either because they died before the super-genes (?) had a chance to express themselves in any practical way, or because those particular genomes did not work well as a whole, the altered genes offsetting the viability and overall health of these *un-realized* specimens).

It also seemed safe to assume that there were many people alive today that possessed this mutated DNA. Many of the individuals that I had already analyzed had died fairly recently, so it was actually inevitable, factoring in *Homo sapiens* reproductive patterns. But would younger *Homo sapiens* possess the mutations? I already knew the answer to that question, but I still had to prove it.

Collecting DNA samples of the dead was inconsequential; of the living, easy enough (actually, extremely easier!), as long as it was done with care. It didn't matter that I was targeting the most influential, most field-relative valuable brains *Homo sapiens* had to offer, for DNA is strewn everywhere carelessly, freely, and in copious amounts, regardless of socioeconomic status or relative professional success. This *Homo sapiens* civilization is still in its infancy as far as DNA technology is concerned, and thus *unconcerned* about leaving its DNA everywhere it roams.

Boston, San Francisco, Los Angeles, Tokyo, Paris, New York, London, Oxford, Orsay, and Rome, they all became my immediate targets, since I would be targeting primarily those involved in formal investigation-based activities. The who's who of scientific research and development on Earth, it would be in these cities where I would be able to quickly test my theory. In fact, the process was a lot simpler, since I did not have to develop the DNA at all. If I wanted to study the brain of a particular *living Homo sapiens*, all I had to do was find myself in their general vicinity, with my morphing unit in *hand*. In this case, however, since I was looking for the presence (or absence) of these super-genes that had mysteriously cropped up after I had last left the planet, I would have to collect actual DNA samples.

MIT was one of the obvious choices, which is what brought me here from Manhattan. I waited outside in Killian Court, one of the grassy areas that dot the campus, facing the Physics Department. I had all the information I needed on all faculty and staff of the Institute. I could name and recognize every one of them. I also knew which of the students were in the list of potential future A-listers, most of whom would be actively involved in the best research projects MIT was sponsoring at the moment, typically overseen by the research fellows, members of the university's faculty.

I was skimming through a book on string theory so as to remain inconspicuous. I was actually enjoying reading firsthand the stumbles that civilizations generally take before discovering the true workings of the meta-universe. Entertaining stuff, mostly; and not surprisingly, sometimes there were even accurate snippets to be found here and there, almost randomly-located throughout the hundreds of pages that attempted to present a theory in vogue, though these snippets were painfully uncommon. To be fair, it was a work in progress, and given the intelligence resources available to the species, a quite powerful of an effort. The advent of advanced computing techniques would very likely accelerate this process of discovery, since that would open up the door to more sophisticated and improved experimentation, which would launch theorists into the ever deeper abysm that is the true nature of the workings of the cosmos.

"But the *peeeeeep* value is all wrong, Dr. Y." Please forgive the censorship, but remember that I must keep the anonymity of anyone that I happen to mention: *Dr. Y* has a real name, of course, and is an actual twenty-first century person, but one which I will not divulge; now, the particular variable name that I assign here could point a keen reader in the right direction, thus the double whammy. Or triple whammy? The world of logic is ripe with paradoxes.

"We don't really know that yet, X." *X* was a twenty-something female student, working with Dr. Y on a very advanced something-or-other. A female *Homo sapiens*, hence I call her X! Dr. Y happened to be male, hence I call him Y. Get it? Couldn't help it... all this DNA slash genome slash chromosome talk gets to me. I apologize. Then again, their gender could be incorrect. I must excuse my obsessively-neurotic effort to shield identities.

"Well, it seems that way to me, especially considering *blank* and *blank* and *blank*. The latter, remember, was a full ten-millionth off the expected value! But I see what you are saying. Too soon to really know for sure. It's frustrating having to wait for Z to finish *his/her* calculations." X seemed to be coming to terms with the inevitable slow pace of cutting-edge research. She would truly practice that skill to death if she lingered on in her chosen field.

They stopped a few paces away from where I was sitting, oblivious of my presence. And why shouldn't they be? I was a nondescript person, reading an undergraduate book on physics, ergo just one more of the plethora of eager-looking students that dot the campus.

The sun was shining bright, as it usually does on cloudless days on Earth, and it was positioned precisely behind them, from my line of sight. As they talked they inadvertently gave me all I needed. I adjusted my electromagnetic sensors and was thus able to clearly follow the path of their tiny DNA-filled droplets that were unintentionally (I would imagine) being launched from their mouth and headed in my direction. The minuscule drops glistened against the dark blue sky not unlike stars in space, and obeyed neat, parabolic paths on their way to the ground. I waited for X and Y to leave (didn't want to be *that* obvious), and collected the samples I needed from both of them by silently instructing a couple of the same kind of robots I had used in Montparnasse—as well as everywhere else where I had gone DNA-fishing—to do the collecting.

I spent the next three hours performing that same task, changing only my location within the Institute, but always outside, on grassy areas. I avoided all eating spots because they are typically more crowded, and I did not need to collect used cups or bottles or plastic silverware (*plastic silver? Ha!*) to achieve my goal; too messy, and hard to avoid looking suspicious when you stick your hands inside garbage cans and pull out dirty stuff only to bag it and carry it away with you, no matter how hard you whistle so as to appear normal, nonchalantly trying to convey the idea that people do such things all the time, on their free time or whatever, as a hobby of sorts...

I walked to Massachusetts Avenue, to the bus stop that is in front of the MIT School of Architecture and Planning, and boarded the number one bus that heads northwest to Harvard Station via the same street. My destination was, of course, Harvard University. I didn't even have to transfer, which was quite welcome. The bus dropped me off across the street from Al's Harvard Square Cafe (not my final destination at the moment), close to the University's Department of Romance Languages and Literatures. A short walk later, I was again surrounded by grass, trees, and walking paths, although this time, I was on Harvard's pristine grounds.

Faculty and students passed by me in fits and starts as their classes cycled, and some would stand or sit close to me as chance would have it. In any case, after a while, I had more than enough DNA samples–properly labeled–for analysis.

Other versions of me were doing the same thing the world over, some having to be more creative than others, especially as the targets became more controversial or high-profile, having to circumvent the security detail that inevitably accompanies such people. Presidents, prime ministers, dictators, I couldn't afford to spare anyone.

But back to my Boston self. I made the five-minute walk to the corner of Waterhouse Street and Garden Street, to the apartment complex that I was renting for my local needs.

I took the stairs to the third floor, took out my key and went inside.

Pris: You are back, Roy. Interesting results. We need to work fast, track down The Reason, The Origin, The Expectation. Boston's DNA edgy enough?

Well, Pris did not exactly *say* this, as *Homo sapiens* understands the action of saying.

It is impossible to communicate to a *Homo sapiens*–even remotely–our exact exchange using any of humanity's communication systems–or combination of systems, for that matter–much less in written form, and so I am forced to translate, to adapt, to conjure up a semi-useful exchange, losing much in the process. As I said before, there is nothing I can do to fix this.

Our quantum sensors exchange waves of probability data that

add what you would term a *je ne sais quois* to our interaction, electromagnetic waves specifically and strategically embedded, another layer of the multifaceted, multidimensional system that advanced civilizations typically use to unequivocally convey precise meaning, tone, purpose, effect, and a plethora of other key components that span the gamut of that which is desired and of that which can be perceived, sensed, experienced, and reasoned: from the trivial to the essential.

Imagine, if you will, somehow integrating physics, math, art (in all of its embodiments), words, light, feelings, senses and voice, simultaneously, and on different levels, during your communication with others... Being able to individually adjust the degree of each and every one of the potential *Homo sapiens*-felt emotions (humor, sadness, joy, surprise, anger, and the rest, as well as the *intellectual* perception of those emotions). Being able to feed data into every sense available. That, and more, is what an advanced communication system is able to do.

I: You did not tell me that you would be here, Pris, though I detected your presence, of course—nothing is wrong with any of my sensors. Boston's DNA is here; I will begin the analysis.

The robots that had stored the DNA samples marched unceremoniously from their compartment at the bottom of my shoe and into the analyzer. A nondescript silver box that could be mistaken for a fancy, minimalist paperweight, silently produced results, which, in turn, were communicated to the project matrix, and thus to us instantly.

Pris was staring out the window, taking in the movement of Cambridge Common Park. Being the middle of summer, the sun was still out, a few hours away from reaching its eventual setting point. A baseball game was leisurely being played out a hundred yards across our building, on the western side of the park, and Pris seemed to be pondering its *raison d'être* (so many answers to that, depending on the level one wished to base the analysis on). Sunlight, shining through Pris' frizzy blond hair, rainbowed into more hues than were seemingly possible. It reminded me of fields of wheat, at dusk, that I'd seen all over planet Earth.

I: It is confirmed. Boston's DNA is mutated as well. The Reason, The Origin, The Expectation... any ideas?

I suspect that most *Homo sapiens*, specifically members of their twenty-first century civilization, are under the impression–or rather *the bias*–that so-called *artificial* intelligent *systems* are unable to perform on par with intelligent organisms that have been–what, created as the result of natural, physical, unintelligent and unintentional forces? Or of the supernatural?

The majority of *Homo sapiens* would say (if only given the chance) that only those species created by magical deities (or its singular version, a *God*) have the ability to create, to be self-aware, to possess free-will. Cue in the concept of soul (or rather inject it, as is the common belief), as humans understand it... So what deities? Take a pick... It does seem to be a crowded category to belong to, not quite an exclusive group if what the plethora of belief-systems seem to vehemently demand that the rest believe are all actually true, never mind the fact that many of them are completely incompatible with each other; what's worse, the possibility of proving the existence of any one of them is outright denied, right from the start, by arguing that only faith should be invoked in matters of any religious beliefs. Quite a convenient set up.

Regardless, it must not be assumed that only DNA-based organisms can accomplish the feat of self-awareness, of invention, of free-will; there are an infinite number of what *Homo sapiens* would probably call life-bearing platforms, or structures, or processing systems, or technologies–out there in the meta-universe–that are capable of achieving it. So, whatever the particular philosophical inclination may be, it must be remembered that forces are forces are forces. It does not matter where they emanate from, they will have the same effect, anywhere in the cosmos, regardless of where they are realizing their potential. Of course, circumstances change, the specific mix of forces change, and certain *local* universal values change, all of which ultimately does have an impact on the end-result. But all else being equal, results can be replicated. And results can be *achieved*.

As it happens, what this *Homo sapiens* species calls consciousness and self-awareness, which it incorrectly assumes is a prerequisite for creativity and intelligence-by the way-can be and is derived from many different computational systems, the life-bearing platforms I just mentioned earlier; in fact, it has been shown that all universal computing systems (regardless of how they specifically operate and what platform they use in order to compute) can be complex enough to the point of deserving to be classified as intelligent. The only relevant variables that must be watched for are internal interaction design and computing power. Thresholds are not clear-cut, however: they vary drastically depending on the processing structure type. Pris and all similar creations are on equal footing with the rest of the lot (those intelligence systems that are the direct by-product of evolutionary forces, such as *Homo sapiens*). After a species crosses a particular threshold, in fact, these civilizations become fully hybrid: they become the product of multiple life-bearing platforms integrated with artificial systems as well. Add to the mix the willful alteration of their existing evolutionary platform, whatever it may be, and the civilization is said to be fully mature, of a type 10+ consciousness.

Pris answered my question.

Pris: Yes. Multiple possibilities, all probable. Discarding the improbable, we are left with three testable theories. Look at the descendant data we have. The mutation is not inherited. Whoever or whatever is doing this, it is clearly an ongoing process, Roy. Connect to proceed.

I truly wish I could convey all that Pris simultaneously included in the exchange: supporting mathematical analysis, quantum probability waves, electromagnetic DNA particle-waves, what humans might call *emotion*-stress markings and values, and the list goes on.

I: I agree. I saw most of it coming from the start, just as you did, Pris. Nice to confirm it, although it's bittersweet. In a second.

I sat down close to the most important piece of equipment I had, the singularity connector. Although I normally had it *within* me, while roaming the Earth, outside of my earthly *homes* or other safe zones, I did not carry it. I could still connect to the metanet, but it was much less efficient since I had to do it via electromagnetic waves that served as a stepping stone leading to the singularity connector itself, which felt (and was) completely different. As drastic as the difference between, say, night and day.

As soon as I touched its metallic surface, I was able to instantly connect to the metanet. It felt good to have direct access once again. Now, it was no longer just Pris and I: all beings that ever were and are, since the metanet was developed, in more universes than can be counted, potentially connected, potentially sharing resources, experiences, creativity, computing power, analytical waves, and anything else that could be transmitted virtually. All via the singularity.

I chose to share certain things, ignoring the irrelevant, hiding that which was necessary. Pris was there, of course, as well as many of my other selves, including my ship-bound version. Pris had already initiated her version of the analysis, and it was wonderfully constructed.

We continued to tweak the resources we had at our disposal, modifying the feedback loops as we deemed fit, and waited for the results. In a matter of minutes, we had what we needed. Although clearly a group effort, *the* final answer came from the brain of—let's call it Adda—whose species had been integrated into the metanet only a recent number of cycles ago, having crossed the necessary civilization threshold that opens up that door. Promising group of individuals, collectively as well, evidently.

Pris: Roy, what's your take on this.

Pris was clearly curious and wanted my explicit perspective, never mind the metanet's version that was *out there*.

I: I side with Adda. Nice setup, by the way. Although my ship-bound version did make that crucial tweak.

I was, of course, trying *to push her buttons,* as *Homo sapiens* often say.

Pris: Jealous of Adda, ergo grasping at straws? Yes, your ship-self is amazing, Roy. Which means what, exactly. That your here-self idolizes your ship-self? How demeaning... you may be barred from the metanet, together with all your other selves.

Pris was, of course, spot-on in her refute. Egos are one of the first things that civilizations need to shed before continuing on in the pursuit of advancing their consciousness-awareness states. No need to continue fighting this already-lost battle. Well, it never had been a battle to begin with. Just a joke that did not target the correct species.

I: I set myself up, and you win.

Pris: Roy, what is happening to you! Earth getting the best of you? There are no winners here. What sort of ego-talk is this?

I: Pris, you really are... good. Switch waves, please. We have to find the microorganism that is causing these mutations. Clearly not a virus, nor a bacterium, as Adda predicts. That leaves not a bacterium, but a group of mutated bacteria, working together. Nothing else works. Barring the improbable, given the data we have collected so far.

Pris: Right. Where do we begin? I suggest finding a recently deceased mutant. We can perform all the tests we need.

Pris was already designing how to do it.

I: Might work. Of course, the mutation could take place during conception, directly on the zygote, in which case we would not find any trace of it on the mutated individual itself.

Pris: I already considered that possibility. We therefore need the parents as well.

I: So we wait for any accidents involving parents and their offspring?

Pris: Yes. I already have three candidates. We don't even have to travel farther than New York. There is one candidate a couple of hours from here, in Connecticut, very close to the New York state line. Let's go.

I: Just the two of us... it will suffice. Let's get my other selves involved. We need more data from their locations. Let's set it up.

The next few minutes, Pris and I worked through the metanet to establish courses of action for all of my other versions. Ship-bound me nudged a few small details, and then we were all on our way.

Pris and I, looking like a regular *Homo sapiens* couple (we even held hands), took the short walk from the apartment building to the Red Line's Harvard Square station, where we took the subway to South Station. We were a bit less than four hours away from our intended destination: Greenwich, Connecticut.

4. Main Asteroid Belt, Solar System

On my last visit to Earth, I had been able to land on the surface of the planet without having to worry about being detected. At all. This time around, things were different. *Homo sapiens* was making strides, carving its name in the backdrop of the cosmos. Technologically, it had been able to discover radar, radio telescopes, satellites, even space-stations for galaxy's sake!, which meant I wouldn't risk trying to reach the planet directly on my transuniversal ship. I could, of course, use shields to blend with whatever my surroundings happened to be, and deflecting radar waves is doable. However, there is always the possibility that something could malfunction, and based on our laws that govern my mission and that prevent me from making our existence known, I would not be risking a planetary landing.

I was thus forced to proceed with an alternate plan. The Main Asteroid Belt that lies between Mars and Jupiter was the obvious choice. I stopped well short of Earth's orbital plane, and joined the millions of rocks that travel around the distant sun in this region of space. I created one independent, physical replicate of myself that would not remain here on the ship, but that was rather sent to Earth–in the company of Pris, of course.

My ship-bound self is what you would call a virtual being. Like the fictitious Hal 9000 from the movie *2001: A Space Odyssey* (I have seen it, of course, as I have seen, read, and studied most of the easily accessible and available media output of the *Homo sapiens* civilization, regardless of its format; from television to film, from printed books to digital files of every protocol designed by the *Homo sapiens* civilization).

Now unlike Hal, I do not become a villain at some point in the story (at least that could never be my computational goal). Part of me (if there is such a thing, for I am a totality, not truly separable into discrete components) resides in the ship's network of computational structures, although it's actually only a temporarily authorized, working link of a Primary Self, which resides in another time, in another universe, physically in the form of contained energy waves, that branches out sensing components as well as additional processing units via the singularity.

For all practical purposes, all of us are one and the same, continuously sharing computations and resources, although there are may exist at times different versions of us, independently experiencing the forces of the meta-universe.

Theoretically, these versions maintain overlapping structures, which are subject to the multidimensional laws of casualty of the meta-universe; in practice, never permanently so (for there is no such thing as simultaneity, no matter how interconnected any group of networks may be; the cosmos operates in many dimensions, with what *Homo sapiens* would probably call multidirectional time and entropy directional arrows).

Pris is also an extension of a version that resides elsewhere, even if Pris is a being that has been purposefully created.

Pris does have specific directives and tendencies that are pre-configured, as needed, on the specific versions that participate on missions such as this one. There are some important differences as far as the individuality of Pris' versions is concerned, but this is not an adequate forum to explain the physical reality and algorithmic philosophy of our collective civilizations, which spans more universes than we care to count, in matters that surpass *Homo sapiens'* current level of technological, social, political, emotional, experiential, biophysical, behavioral, and intellectual development.

After randomly selecting Roy's *Homo sapiens* persona, Roy and Pris boarded the interplanetary vehicle and went on their way, successfully reaching the surface of planet Earth, only after taking a short detour to the Moon; it was necessary to explore Apollo's lunar landing sites and all the debris left behind during their missions; I am nothing if not thorough.

As for ship-bound me, everything on the ship, or rather, the ship itself, is an extension of this ship-bound self. Through the network of sensors, whatever happens to the ship, regardless of its un-connectedness, is immediately *felt* by me. Quantum sensors at play, something that to a twenty-first century *Homo sapiens* reader, may be able to picture it somehow. If only in an intuitive fashion.

I sensed an approaching miniature asteroid, and adjusted the course accordingly. No need to humor the rock's desire to collide with me (I would have to perform maneuvers such as this thousands of times before the mission was over; very minor, trivial stuff).

Waiting around was not, strictly speaking, necessary. As I have already stated by now, all of my Earth-bound selves (as well as Pris) have access to the metanet. But it is necessary to have in my possession all relevant physical samples that would be collected during the mission. These could not be sent using a similar concept of what Earth currently considers quantum teleportation, creating exact replicas of the originals anywhere in the meta-universe, because the process would alter the living samples to the point of being worthless. A strict no-no in the field of alien life research, given that minute quantum crystallizations pile up uncontrollably.

I was aware of the recent developments, of course. Mutated *Homo sapiens* DNA. Interference of civilizations that are deemed *Quarantined-Independent* is not allowed. But the meta-universe is not perfect. Nor is the collective, voluntary alliance I am part of. Forces are forces are forces. Nothing else is absolute in the meta-universe.

I had sensors that came in handy at times like these. My Earth-bound versions (as well as Pris, singular) would be at a loss without me in this respect. I altered the design of a few of my readily available in-ship components, creating from scratch those that were not already physically present using data-waves that came straight from the metanet, and took to scanning the Solar system. I backed away and spanned all its width and breadth, and after a while detected remanent gravity waves, the by-product of the bending of the fabric of the cosmos, that could only have come from an interstellar ship, having boldly emanated a few kilometers above the surface of Mars (protocol deems the process to be initiated at a much safer distance *away* from a massive object such as the planet Mars). They were less than twelve hours old.

It would seem logical to assume that whoever was causing the mutations had detected my presence and had probably decided to cancel the ensuing and potentially quite awkward encounter of (two?) locally-alien beings.

But Earth is a big planet, and it is densely populated by more organisms than can be counted; a biodiversity that is decent enough (at least that's how it was for millions of years up until *Homo sapiens* recently began to have a *negative* impact on this particular planetary statistic–which, by the way–seems to be getting exponentially worse, barring an unprecedented, collaborative effort that would appear to be impossible to implement given this species' current psychosociological traits).

Back to the gravitational waves... something or someone had fled, that much was clear. I doubt the ship and its contents would be hanging around, hiding somewhere in the vicinity of the Solar System. I saw no reason for that, but in hindsight, *reasonable* reasons can suddenly materialize, *that* I know as well, while in foresight, nonce can be seen. It would be very hard to find it if it was still in this star system somewhere, but not *absolutely* impossible either.

As to whether or not there is someone or something—to acknowledge *Homo sapiens'* crude distinction between the innate and the organic, really quite unnecessary, if you must know—still roaming around Earth, one or many, regardless of the whereabouts of its ship, I'd say the likelihood is close to being a certainty. A genetic alteration effort of this type and magnitude tells me that there is an enormous vested interest in accomplishing whatever whomever's goal may be. Abandoning it all simply because of my presence would not seem a very likely scenario.

After learning of my findings and musings, my Earth-bound versions—as well as Pris—were not surprised; they in fact shared my point of view.

Having finished scanning all major bodies in this star system, and after seeding strategically-placed gravitational wave detectors, which would allow me to instantly register the presence of any non-*Homo sapiens* vessel moving about (in other words, excluding those of Earth origin that I knew roamed the star system, of which I possessed a full list, and which did generate, if minute, gravity waves as well, regardless of its propulsion technology), I returned to the asteroid belt, opting for a different location. My gravity waves would give me away, so the last four thousand miles were travelled without using my regular thrusters, opting for the much slower, but untraceable, ship-produced gamma emissions. They were indistinguishable from any star's gamma ray production, including, of course, that of the this system's star that we were orbiting.

I would reduce my activity to the point of matching the surrounding's average energy output, just to be on the safe side, which meant that I would have to slow down and thinly spread out all communications with Earth. It was a small price to pay.

The bulk of the mission would thus be in the collective hands of Pris and my Earth-bound physical selves.

I couldn't wait to find out what in star's name was going on.

5. Connecticut

The train ride had been completely uneventful. Pris and I had kept our interactions within the guidelines of the average *Homo sapiens* local couple: talking, of course, holding hands, displaying all the right emotions and physical interactions. Fortunately, because we were in such close proximity, nothing prevented us from using our quantum sensors, which allowed us to continue to interact efficiently in order to work on the problems encountered on this mission. Had this not been the case, we would have had to use electromagnetic waves; they are very slow and cumbersome to use in comparison.

Pris and I had learned from my spaceship-bound self that a ship had departed from Mars shortly after our arrival; we therefore expected to be in the presence of an alien being (or beings?), the plural being more likely. This at the planetary level, of course, and not necessarily on the train we happened to be riding in at the moment. As a precaution, we scanned all the train's cars to determine if there were any anomalies that we could detect, which did produce two positive results.

Mainly, Pris and I, of course!

We got off the train in Stamford, CT, since its next stop would leave us farther away from our final destination (it would have taken us all the way to Manhattan's Penn Station, to be precise).

It was one thirty in the morning, too late to take the MTA line to the town of Greenwich, since there weren't any trains that would be running this line for another three hours, so we were forced to hire one of the Yellow Cab taxis that were leisurely waiting by the south parking area. We asked to be driven to Greenwich Hospital, and were there less than twenty-five minutes later.

At this time of night, we knew that only the Emergency Room entrance would be open, having checked its hours of operation, specifically, given the local time, its after-hours policies. We asked the cab driver to drop us off in the ER, paid the fare and gave him a generous tip, promising to double it if he waited for us while we took care of our pending business. Pris and I then headed inside.

A security officer was sitting behind a desk, reading the newspaper. She looked up, waiting for us to explain our presence, since we were not, as far as was immediately visually obvious, injured.

"Good evening, officer. My wife needs medical assistance. May we talk to the attending doctor, please?"

"May I see both of your ID's?"

I handed her our driver licenses (both from the state of Connecticut, having created them with our morphing unit during the cab ride specifically in view of this impending need), and waited for her to register us in the system.

She printed our black and white sticky labels and asked us to sit down in the waiting area. We really didn't need to push things by putting on a show in order to get *immediate* attention. After all, the bodies of the three victims, being already dead, would not be moved anywhere until morning (at least according to the data logged in the hospital's computer network, in which we had easily installed a bot hours ago to help us with our mission).

A few minutes later, a surprisingly very much awake nurse walked out of the ER corridor and called our number from behind the counter.

"Good evening... are you the ER doctor?" Pris asked, knowing perfectly well that she was a nurse.

"Good evening, ma'am. No, I am the triage nurse. I will notify the physician as soon as I know more about your condition. What is your emergency?" Although she didn't actually snap, she was a bit on the defensive, without really being able to control it. It was what Pris wanted to achieve with her question: nothing elicits a lowering of the guard more than triggering feelings of remorse.

"I think I just had a miscarriage." Pris reddened her eyes for effect, increasing the moisture just enough to force a tiny tear to materialize, making the nurse feel guilty. And that she did accomplish.

"I am terribly sorry," the nurse said, truly feeling it, reaching out to stroke the side of her arm, making what she knew perfectly well was just a feeble attempt to comfort her.

"It's okay, thank you. I will get through this," Pris replied.

"Please come with me. You can join us, of course," she said, looking at me directly.

We followed her into one of the available private rooms (there seemed to be plenty of empty ones at this time of night), where she asked Pris to lay down on the gurney. I stood next to her, playing the supporting role of the supporting partner, pretending to be too dumbstruck to say a word. The nurse looked at me as if pleased with my behavior, slightly nodding approvingly.

"You can call me Sophie, Mrs. Kane. I am going to check your blood pressure, pulse, and temperature. This will only take a minute."

The ER nurse almost kept her promise; fifty-five seconds later she left the room to get the physician. The fact that she didn't rush out meant she had determined that Pris was stable, which is what we wanted.

I waited a few seconds before walking out of the room. I went straight to the hospital's morgue, which was located two floors below the ER. Pris had programmed and activated the virtual *bot* in the hospital's computer network, which was now granting me access anywhere I went, while erasing every trace of our presence (admission records, editing all video recordings, and replacing all software pointers to their original state—thus effectively purging our digital existence from the hospital's network).

As soon as I was inside the morgue, I scanned the room looking to match the numbers that Pris had given me. These were etched on the lower left corner of the stainless steel doors, and quickly found them: compartments five, seven, and nine. Evidently, whoever had stowed the bodies had decided to place them strategically having clearly been emotionally affected by their untimely deaths: father to the left, eleven year old son in the middle, mother on the right, all next to each other.

I pulled the sheets aside, and checked the wrist and ankle bands to confirm their identity: Richard Laisset, the father; Karen Laisset, the mother; and Ben Laisset, the son. I started with the son first, because I needed to confirm our theory (that he was, in fact, a DNA mutant). Having checked his school records and achievements, Pris had assured me that he would be.

One of the insect-sized robots that I was in possession of swiftly obtained a sample, and went straight into the analyzer that I had brought with me so that the DNA could be tested on the spot.

"You were right, Pris." I said to her (well, I *communicated* to her, without using the *Homo sapiens'* spoken word).

I put the sheet back on the child's body, pushed the tray all the way inside, and closed the door. Now, I would have to work intensively on the other two bodies. Would I find something, anything, that would give away the mutation process that was being used?

I started with the mother, trying to prove or disprove one of the theories that we had collectively come up with in the apartment back in Boston.

I sent three robots into the mother's body. One went to the left ovary, one to the right. Both of these would be taking samples of oogonia, oocytes, and hopefully ova cells. The third robot went straight to the hypothalamus, a region of the brain that we believed could house what we were looking for (at least according to one more of the multiple theories we had come up with).

Before I moved on to the last body, Pris suggested I send in a fourth robot, this time to take bone marrow specimens from the femur, with the directive to acquire samples of the more than twenty cell types that are typically found in this structure. I knew why she had made the request, and although it was a long shot, I obliged. What was the harm?

I then moved on to the father, and sent in the four robots as well. The goal was to obtain samples of the spermatogonia and spermatocytes cells specific to the male *Homo sapiens*, and from the hypothalamus and bone marrow, the latter common to both males and females of the species.

Less than ten minutes later, I had finished coordinating the sampling process. I covered the two adult bodies and slid the trays back inside the refrigerator, firmly closing the doors.

At the suggestion of a non-local processing structure that was part of the project matrix, I opened tray nine once again and removed cells from the developing boy's reproductive organs, which could prove useful later on. Less than two minutes later, I had all that was needed at this stage of the proceedings.

As I was leaving, Pris warned me that she could see from the video captured by one of the security cameras that someone was walking outside the morgue's corridor: it was a male security officer performing one of his multiple rounds of the night. We knew that if the person followed proper procedures, this would be an inevitable stop in his route. Evaluating our options, which included preventing the electronic key from granting him access to the morgue (easily accomplished since we could control anything that was connected to the hospital's computer network), we finally decided on a course of action that would prevent, as much as possible, even the slightest possibility of a physical confrontation between the guard and myself. The bot easily triggered a fire alarm in one of the storage rooms that branched to the left of the corridor, leading him away from the morgue, knowing the security officer would have to head there immediately.

Pris confirmed that I was free to return to her side, which I promptly did. The physician had already talked to her, and was in the process of ordering some tests from the ER's charting and support center, partially blocked from view from where we were.

We went into the hallway and told the ER nurse that we were leaving.

"What? Why? We need to make sure you are okay, Mrs. Kane. I cannot let you go."

"I understand, and I appreciate your concern. But you already checked my vitals, and the doctor confirmed that I am not bleeding anymore. I will see my OB/GYN first thing in the morning, I promise."

I chimed in. "But honey, are you sure this is the right thing to do? I understand how you feel, but please, we need to make sure that you are okay. Let's at least inform the doctor..." I had to say this, knowing how the average *Homo sapiens* male psyche would respond to the current set of circumstances.

The nurse looked at me, and agreed. "Listen to your husband, Mrs. Kane." She even held Pris' arm, slightly pressuring her to return to her room.

"No. I made up my mind. None of you know what I am going through right now, and I have to tell you, this is making it much worse. I want to go home, and that is exactly what I am going to do. Nothing will happen to me. I know my body... I have been living with it for more than thirty years. Thank you, nurse *peeeeep*, but we are leaving the hospital right now. You have my insurance information, so I am free to go."

Pris grabbed my hand and dragged me towards the exit.

"Thank you... I do apologize for the inconvenience. Please explain everything to the doctor," I said to the nurse, as I was half-dragged by Pris, lagging one step behind her as I talked to the nurse.

We knew the taxicab was in fact waiting for us outside. It was easily detectable by many of our sensors.

We were anxious to have the results of the samples we had collected, but we were not carrying the necessary equipment with us, so we would just have to wait. Because we were so much closer to Manhattan than to Boston, we requested the driver to take us there at once. He did not seem to mind. He quoted us a fare that we did not even question, and were soon being driven down I-95, south-bound.

I was also aware, of course, that Deborah might be meeting me for coffee less than six hours from now, in Manhattan. I would certainly try to be there if I could. It was certainly not a priority, but if I could fit that in to my schedule, I certainly would.

6. West Village, NY

Our collective efforts were paying off. During the last three hours, we had made great strides towards discovering the truth behind the controlled gene mutations that had been taking place in selected individuals of the *Homo sapiens* species for more than 550 years. With the samples Pris and I had acquired, as well as those obtained by my other selves in three hundred and thirty-five cities across the planet, a very clear picture was beginning to emerge. We had even taken samples from our own bodies, with surprising results.

Back in Manhattan since the pre-dawn hours, I was only five minutes away from the coffee shop where I had asked Deborah to meet me. It was now 10:37 a.m., so I left Pris and headed there.

It was a short two-block walk down Greenwich Street, headed north, where I then turned left onto Charles Street. The coffee shop is adjacent to the corner building, set in the ground floor of a five-story, red-brick apartment complex. A couple of benches served patrons wishing to remain outdoors while enjoying their favorite brew, weather permitting, of course. They were currently empty.

I walked in a few minutes before the agreed-upon time. Although I had been in here only twice before, the barista recognized me immediately.

"Good morning, Roy! Good to have you back! Your usual?" he asked me, legitimately happy to see me. He was certainly good at his job, due mostly because he seemed to enjoy it.

"Good morning! Yes, please. By the way, did a woman by the name of Deborah leave a message for me?"

"No. But let me double check." He went inside the kitchen located on the back, where he disappeared for less than twenty seconds. When he came back to the front, he told me that no one with that name had called this morning.

I figured Deborah would be arriving soon, otherwise she would have at least called to cancel. I had not pegged her as the type of person that would change her mind without a warning, and I was usually very good making those kind of predictions.

I sat down on a high table next to the window, sipping my triple-espresso, and waited for Deborah to arrive. It was not particularly busy this morning; there were only two people inside (not counting me, since I am not a *Homo sapiens*, and thus humbly excuse myself from the collective word of *people*). A twenty-something college student, which was a quite obvious fact if one only took into consideration her reading material (an advanced-level chemistry brick that very few *Homo sapiens* would read for the leisure of it on a Saturday morning); the other person was a teenage-looking male listening to music with his earphones on, eyes closed, drumming the song's beat with a pair of imaginary sticks (and doing a terrible job of it, by the way... I could, at will, filter and amplify the sound emanating from the tiny speakers in his ears, or read the electromagnetic signals that his phone was generating-whatever happened to be best –allowing me the privilege of analyzing his *asynchronous* performance).

At this time, my Tokyo self was logging in the results of the samples acquired a few minutes ago, so I paid attention to that update. The information did not surprise me.

We had now conclusive evidence of what was to blame for the mutations: a three step process had been specifically developed, using mutated bacteria, that had now infected most—if not all —*Homo sapiens*—and *only Homo sapiens*—in the planet. Not surprisingly this actually included ourselves (all Earth Roys, and Pris)!

The once mutated *and* continually mutating bacteria have a simple directive. Bacterium A produces a particular set of enzymes that seek out specific gene markers inside the host's gamete DNA. If detected, the enzymes alter their folded shape, which bacterium B reacts to only when all of the markers are present. Once this happens, bacterium B releases viral vectors that is designed to alter the DNA of the gamete cell, effectively mutating it, at the locations which other enzymes produced by this bacterium adhere to. Finally, bacterium C works with a time delay: in the presence of one of the enzymes produced by bacterium B, it will slowly produce clean-up proteins that neutralize and decompose all of the enzymes created by bacteria A and B, ending the cycle.

Ingenious, advanced, and clearly not a *Homo sapiens* technology. This was perfectly in line with one of the more feasible theories that we had collectively foreseen, but still an alarming prospect none the less.

I looked outside and saw Deborah crossing the street, headed towards the coffee shop. I slid off the stool and opened the door just as she was about to open it. The glare hadn't allowed her to see me inside getting the door for her, so she stumbled and almost fell to the ground as she applied a forward-momentum force to a door that pulled away from her. Not what I had intended.

"I'm sorry, Deborah. Are you alright?" I asked her.

"Is this payback for last time?" she answered back, smiling, straightening her blouse as she regained her composure.

"No-no-no… I know why it would seem that way, but you have to believe me, I was only trying to get the door for you. Are you alright?"

She looked at me with a quizzical look on her face. "Yes. I am fine. Well, here I am. I always order their espresso here, I just love it. What are you having?"

"The same... I already ordered mine. After all, I didn't know if you were going to show up at all. That blow without caffeine in my system would have been simply too much."

"A bit insecure, are we?"

"Well, you never know, do you. I figured you would have called to let me know you weren't coming, though, had that been the case. I didn't peg you as been *that* mean," I smiled as I said this, winking playfully.

She seemed to delay a response purposefully, but I could not be sure. It had happened too fast, and had caught me off guard, so even my quantum sensors were of no help.

"So, about that coffee... I need my caffeine, Roy!"

"Oh, right! Let me get it for you. I did promise it would be my treat."

I ordered her a triple espresso, which in hindsight, should have made me suspicious (what were the chances that she would order that exact same drink?). I carefully brought it to her.

"Would you like to walk outside with me? It is a lovely day, and I would really hate to waste it by staying cooped up inside an air-conditioned coffee shop."

"Sure. Where to?"

"We can take a stroll down Greenwich Street. Head towards Greenwich Avenue. Do some window shopping. It'll be fun. Come on."

She stood up, coffee in hand, and waited for me to follow her. And so I did.

I waved goodbye to the barista, and headed outside.

There were a few clouds way up high in the sky, but nothing to really prevent the sun from bathing everything in sight. And although the temperature was eighty-eight degrees, it was the compensating cooler breeze blowing from the east that made it feel less than that. I am, of course, immune to these nuances, since I am able to adjust my internal temperature precisely by changing my metabolism rates and efficiently dissipating or generating heat as needed, without the need to actually sweat. Only in extreme temperature conditions would I be truly affected, outside of the endurable by living organisms that are DNA-based.

Deborah seemed to be immune to the sun's warmth as well, since she chose to walk on the west side of Greenwich street, headed uptown, which did not provide any shadow at this time of day. I did take note of this, but did not really act on it. In hindsight, this should have warned me that something was wrong. But then again, the stores on this side of the street might have been preferable to those on the other side, or she could have been filling up on her vitamin D, or any of an endless plausible reasons that needn't have concerned me. Hindsight crystallizes only one outcome, though. And I *could have* seen it coming, I *could have* prepared better for it.

"So what do you do, Roy?" she asked me, probably to break the silence, which had actually been enjoyable. Not awkward at all.

"I write. Mostly for other people."

"You mean you are... what they call a professional ghostwriter?" She pretended to struggle recollecting the term. I did find that odd, unnecessary, but shrugged it off for the time being. Processing algorithms are triggered by innumerable variables, so how could I know what had activated that bizarre response?

"Yes," I answered.

"Must be depressing... sorry, I probably shouldn't have said that."

"It's okay. I welcome an honest, challenging conversation; it is refreshing, truth be told. Besides, please don't be offended, but it is not the first time I've been told that. But why do you think it must be depressing? I'm not yet question your argument..."

"Well, because if you have the ability to write, to transmit ideas, paint scenarios, create interesting worlds, why limit yourself to what others want, to what others dictate? Don't you want to do your own thing? Wouldn't you prefer to impact the universe as you so choose?" Deborah had remained calm throughout the exchange. Odd, given the context and the words. Third clue that in hindsight, I *could have* paid attention to.

"But I do have an impact on the universe through my writing, never mind through the obvious ways in which we all do. Even if others do specify a general goal, I get to do with it pretty much what I want. I can even alter their intended message and at the same time make it seem like I complied, when in reality, unconsciously, readers will be able to know what I really meant."

"Still, I think it's better to just do your own thing, and let the universe know that it is you who is doing it."

That was the second time she used the word universe, all under a two-minute span. Fourth *warning* I did not heed.

When we got to the corner of Greenwich Street and Perry Street, I followed her as she crossed the intersection diagonally, and began walking on the north-side of Perry. Some outfit or other was working on the building's facade, hence the scaffold that surrounded the entire structure, providing us pedestrians with a cover that began a mere two feet above my head. There was a white, medium-sized moving truck parked on the left side of the street, effectively creating an improvised and probably unintentional tunnel in that small section of the sidewalk.

In hindsight, Deborah had maneuvered things so that I ended up being closest to the street, and hence to the white truck's side.

"And what is it that you do, Deborah? I promise not to be too aggressive with your profession." She never answered back; in retrospect, her subsequent actions provided an answer, clearer than the purest of vacuums anywhere. The truck's side door was already open, and the instant we approached it, Deborah pushed me inside. My quantum sensors, clearly under attack, went berserk as I began to mount my defense, rendering me completely helpless, powerless to counter-attack. The data received after that moment, which only lasted for 1.8 seconds at that, was utterly useless. All unintelligible nonsense.

I never heard from that version of myself again.

7. Manhattan, NY

Pris realized something had gone wrong, not because my Manhattan self had stopped communicating, because those interruptions do take place from time to time for a number of reasons, but because during what was ultimately *the* final transmission, the quantum data had been completely corrupted. This was, inherently, a quantum impossibility had my Manhattan self remained even partially operational. Only the complete destruction of the entangled data source could explain the information Pris had received.

Repeated efforts to make contact with that version of myself, both from Pris and from my ship-bound self, failed utterly. That particular version of me had not been in possession of a singularity connector, as was the custom when wandering about Earth's crowded streets, but that did not mean we couldn't try to communicate using electromagnetic waves. However, we did not pick up even the tiniest of signals. Being tied to metabolic activity which was part of that body's design, this meant Manhattan Roy was no longer functional (the word dead applies, as *Homo sapiens* understands it).

We all knew that our secret had been compromised. It was now out there, roaming planet Earth, in the hands of one or more beings (obviously the latter, given the alarming reports we were all getting from the rest of my Earth-bound selves). It also made perfect sense to assume that whoever had done this to

Manhattan Roy was also behind the mutations, and was responsible for the simultaneous attacks that were taking place against my other selves worldwide. That meant, of course, that they (if plural) were thus not of Earthly origin, since the technology needed to carry out these actions was simply too advanced.

They were beings from another civilization that had blatantly invaded an interfered with an off-limits galaxy, planet, civilization, and with the alien surveyors to boot (Pris and all my versions of me, that is). Legally, quite a string of no-no's, under a meta-universal framework, of course; Earth's laws come up empty-handed vis-a-vis alien civilization meddling.

We could not yet know what Deborah was. Although the brain quantum scan that Manhattan Roy had performed did correspond to a *Homo sapiens* brain, that did not prove a thing. Replicating a body of this species is simple, controlling it easier still, and thus we could not know for sure if Deborah was extraterrestrial, or a *Homo sapiens* hire (willing or unwilling, either a true possibility).

Pris acted quickly. She packed the samples and the singularity connector, as well as anything else that could compromise our otherworldliness, stuffed everything in a backpack, and left the apartment for good, knowing that to return would be reckless, to say the least. We simply had to assume that whoever had killed Manhattan Roy knew about this place, and so it could no longer be treated as a safe zone.

Pris was on high alert. Metabolically speaking, it meant going into hyper-drive; certain chemicals would have to be consumed at a much faster pace, which meant that sourcing them would be critical in order to maintain a consistent level of performance; even taking into account the technologically advanced metabolic processes that governed our ad-hoc gene design, sourcing these nutrients would be a primary concern.

Pris scanned everything in sight. Data overload was never an issue, given the design of Pris' processing systems and sensor interconnectivity. Built in structural rules would prevent this from ever happening.

By the time Pris was out of the building's stairwell and headed towards the lobby, the physical transformation had been complete: she was no longer a blonde, eye color now a dark hazel, cheekbones less pronounced but the chin more dominant now, and a full five inches taller. It was now impossible to say that the Pris that exited the stairwell on the ground floor looked anything like the Pris that had entered it on the third floor.

Pris was careful to delete all of the building's public surveillance video recordings, adding a level of protection to what would have been clearly an alien metamorphosis taking place in plain digital sight.

Once on the sidewalk, Pris turned left and walked towards the corner of 7th Avenue and Bedford Street, turned left again on Christopher Street and turned right on Hudson Street. Pris was walking fast, because we feared that the truck could be on the move.

As soon as Pris started walking down Hudson, the rear part of the truck came into view; it was indeed leaving the place where Roy had been deactivated, and was now being driven up Hudson towards 8th Avenue.

Pris was capable of running six times faster than the average *Homo sapiens*, but to do that here would be too risky. Online local reports did not bode well for us: there weren't any traffic jams in the general area, which meant that we would probably lose them if Pris remained walking at the current pace.

On the other hand, taking control of a vehicle (borrowing it, in other words), was a simple matter.

Pris located a keyless entry, keyless ignition vehicle in the vicinity, a silver-colored BMW sedan, unlocked the door, and went inside. For the start button to work, the appropriate electromagnetic signal had to be emulated, which Pris promptly emitted.

Before long, Pris was driving up Hudson Street, careful not to break any traffic laws, but in close pursuit of the white truck, still too far away to detect any of the typical signals that emanate from *Homo sapiens* beings, although something organic was definitely inside, that much was detectable even at the distance that currently separated them.

Half a block ahead of Pris, the truck veered sharply to the right onto Bleecker Street, now headed south. Pris followed as fast as possible without running over anyone or hitting another vehicle, of course, successfully catching up to it. Once Pris was side by side with the truck, Pris used electromagnetic signals to interrupt the truck's on-board computer, stalling the engine. However, at this point we realized that we had been played. There were two beings that were organic-based inside the truck's cabin, but clearly not *Homo sapiens...* instead, they were both *Canis lupus familiaris*.

But was Manhattan Roy's inert body in the back?

Pris swerved in front of the truck, got off the car and headed to the side door located towards the rear. As Pris walked past the cabin area, we noticed that the truck had been operated by remote control; there were crudely designed levers and other mechanical devices that had been used to maneuver it. The dogs that were inside the main cabin had been there simply to throw us off the scent. The irony was not lost on us at all.

Some of the other drivers were blowing their horns as they drove around the newly-created obstruction, in keeping with the city's infamous driving etiquette, though most of them ignored what was apparently just another vehicle that had chosen to break down in the middle of the road. They all seemed to be bored, disillusioned, even, by the lack of crushed metal to be morbidly analyzed, or by the absence of any accident victims to gawk at.

Pris found the rear door unlocked, which did not surprise us. However, it was closed, which meant that we could not know what waited inside. Not wanting to risk anything, we deployed a robot that went from Pris' arm to the truck's metal side. It found its way to the truck's interior through a small gap formed between the door and the truck's frame, and once inside, we were able to determine that it was safe to enter.

Pris slid the door open. Except for Manhattan's Roy shirt which was lying on the container's floor, the cargo area was completely empty.

Pris swiftly scanned the shirt, and detected something on the left pocket; Pris reached for the USB flash drive that had been left inside, having identified its distinctive–and obvious–design. A crude and very rudimentary way to store data–or to pass on a message to her, perhaps?–but clearly relevant.

Pris put it away inside her backpack.

"Step out of the truck with your hands in the air right now!"

Pris turned around and saw a police officer, one hand in the holster, looking dead serious.

"Yes officer."

Pris slowly got off the side of the truck, arms in the air. "What is the problem, officer?"

"Turn around! Slowly! And put your hands against the truck! Now!"

We realized that playing along would not be in our best interest. We both came up with the best course of action (it did not matter that I was in the ship, millions of miles away from Manhattan... we were working together as these events unfolded, our quantum communication effectively instantaneous at the distance that separated us).

We are not supposed to interfere with the beings of Earth, except under very specific conditions. And this was one of them. Pris sent a paralyzing electromagnetic pulse that targeted the officer's parietal lobe, and left the scene, walking calmly, as if nothing had happened.

The officer was not harmed, and was unable to remember

anything that had taken place a full minute before regaining his composure. His report would thus state that when he arrived, he found two abandoned vehicles, save for the German Shepherd dogs that were inside one of them, specifically, inside the truck's cabin.

Pris headed uptown to Penn Station, located on 7th Avenue and W31st, about thirty blocks from where she was, not wanting to risk being inside a vehicle of any kind (taxicab, bus, or *borrowed* car).

In order to remain undetected, Pris would have to go offline immediately. By now, she had learned that she was practically alone in the planet, and so it didn't really matter. I would thus be out of the loop until Pris deemed it safe to connect to the metanet once again.

I knew Pris would not leave the island of Manhattan, for it was best to remain in the city, find a place to stay, and try to figure out what in star's name was going on from that specific geographical location, since it was probably in the city were Pris would be able to find the clues we desperately needed.

8. The Allegiance

As the events that were taking place on Earth were relayed via the singularity to the metanet, ultimately to what I will coin for the purposes of this autobiography the *CPU* (information which was being transmitted by my ship-bound version, of course), rules were being created and action matrices were being designed. I could choose to ignore them, of course, but that could potentially result in undesired consequences to my Primary Self, something to avoid as much as possible. If, on the other hand, I kept with the program, my Primary Self would remain unscathed, a primary directive.

The acronym I coined, CPU, stands for "Central Processing *Unity*"; now, I know very well that *Homo sapiens* already possesses a version of it—mainly, the "Central Processing *Unit*" that runs all of their twenty-first century gadgets.

It is what some on Earth would call *serendipitous* how these things align themselves. For this *Homo sapiens* civilization's version of a CPU can be used to describe the resulting entity of the civilizations that have come together under a single Allegiance, of which I am a part of, by the simple act of adding a single letter, in this case, the 'y', assuming, of course, that the English language is known.

And thus the new acronym becomes a word-play version of the older, the meaning of the latter enhanced by the meaning of the former.

This Allegiance is in fact a unity (and you might also say a unit!), and we do process information. As for the word "central", it applies and it doesn't, depending on the philosophical framework that one wishes to use. For we are in fact a centralized civilization, in the sense that all of us who belong to it–regardless of where we happen to branch off to and spend our energy experiencing *computations*–remain linked together through the singularity, regardless of the fact that the allegiance does not occupy a centralized position is space-time. Although the allegiance is everywhere, there does exist a virtual centralized set of processes that allow us to share information, computations, energy, and resources.

We ourselves are a collection of beings that vary in type, origin, form, shape, substance, chemistry, virtuality, chirality, matter and antimatter type, history, space-time presence, energy scale, dimensional presence, consciousness type, and computational mechanisms (quantum, chemical, physical, electrical, magnetic, or combinations thereof). It would be impossible to classify all of us individual units, let alone name each and every one of us. Never mind the fact that in the allegiance nothing is static. Everything fluctuates, and hence, so does the allegiance itself.

Units morph as need be (depending on their type) or as they themselves desire (such as my Primary Self, who is a particularly active *morpher*), based on stimuli that comes from the playing field: the collection of meta-universes that comprises all that there is, including, of course, chance, random quantum crystallizations, unentanglement processes that allow the meta-universe to be nondeterministic. For without the latter, we would all be following a *simple* perfectly defined script.

For every wave-particle and space-time component that exists is actually following a script, but the script is *anything but* simple. Only in hindsight are all actions and all events determined; but not so in foresight... the quintessential source of free will that all civilizations struggle to comprehend during their early evolutionary stages of their philosophical understanding of the workings of the cosmos comes from a mix of the inherent randomness of the meta-universe and of the inevitable fact that the system–that is, the cosmos itself–is non-reducible. There is no single set of rules that reduces the computational effort required to predict the future other than the complete list of rules that actually *do* govern the meta-universe. The only way to truly *and* completely know what will happen is to simply observe how the meta-universe *determines* it, by allowing the cosmos itself (as if any entity or collection of entities could ever stop it!) to execute its rules given the specific constraints that would play a factor in the given scenario. There is simply no other way.

The Allegiance is in possession of innumerable peripherals and computational structures, including systems that store information, systems that process information, and systems that keep all of the units and the peripherals interconnected, primarily via the singularity, which permeates and supports all of the fabric of space and time that constitutes the physical dimensions of the meta-universe. The Allegiance is an extremely rich source of computational potential, and its primary directive is to serve all units that form part of it, and to protect all future members of the Allegiance, regardless of their evolutionary stage, from computational cessation.

As I relayed the events to the Allegiance, certain units chose to get involved in the computation and analysis of the situation, and we collectively assigned specific computational processes that were currently available to aid me in this mission. As it happened, my Primary Self was occupied in other matters of which I did not have access to, and so was unable to participate full force in these proceedings.

First, the metanet confirmed that the Allegiance was not responsible for these events (a highly unlikely possibility, but we still had to eliminate it from the list). All this meant, however, was that nobody from the Allegiance was officially involved–to put it in earthly terms (though not exactly equivalent, close enough for the sake of this argument). There could still be a unit or group of units, members of the Allegiance, acting on their own. This was a possibility that we had no way of proving or disproving just yet.

We needed more information.

The second realistic option was that a unit or a group of units belonging to one (or more) of the many civilizations that have chosen to remain independent of the Allegiance were responsible for the actions taking place on Earth. And this did appear to be the most likely scenario, biased as the conclusion may seem.

Of course, there was a third alternative: mix the first and the second theories, and voilá, another plausible scenario is now on the list. All other options were discarded because we determined that they were nearly impossible, statistically speaking, to deserve our attention, at least for now. Simply too far-fetched.

The theories and the circumstances provided the input that we required; the knowledge possessed by the allegiance, the innumerable laws, histories, and experiences, these provided the reference set; and the analytical/logical design of the computational structures served as the philosophical framework that allowed us to design a plan. Before we could begin to put into action, however, we had to wait for Pris to make contact with us again. For it was determined that Pris would now be in charge. A logical choice, considering that she was specifically created with such a purpose in mind.

9. Offline Pris

Pris knew that just as Manhattan Roy–as well as the others–had been deactivated, the same thing could happen to her (not a pronoun I'd like to use, since Pris is not really a female, just as I am not really a male, but the limitations of *Homo sapiens* speech leave me no choice, which stem, of course, from our abysmally different realities).

Not that Pris would let that happen willingly: deactivation of a Non Primary Self requires adequate preparation and timing in order to avoid loss of information as well as undesirable sensations, feelings and experiences. Additionally, Pris had never experienced it, and was in no rush to live through it.

Earth-bound Roys had felt only the cosmos knows what during the instant before ceasing to exist; even though the information was never transmitted to anything or anyone, the experience *happened* and had been very real to those specific beings. Period. Computations had taken place. The allegiance did lose not only about half an hour's worth of full experiential data, probably not very critical (but who can really say?), but also (and perhaps more importantly) half an hour's worth of computations that will never be accessible. Multiplied, of course, by the number of Earth-bound Roys that had been destroyed.

Manhattan Roy, for example, had been a unique being, experiencing a unique set of circumstances, and crystallizing a unique set of quantum values, all the while performing unique computations, which are now lost in space-time, "*like tears in the rain*" (to borrow the words penned by Rutger Hauer for the movie Blade Runner, which I have also seen). Manhattan Roy was as unique as every other being, unit, organism, or computational creation that can exist.

Pris wanted to ensure that she remained safe from harm, first and foremost. Probably facing beings at least as advanced as us (technologically speaking, if not ethically and morally so), she had decided to scan her body for any signs of markers, transmitters, or space-time disruptors that could give her position away.

As soon as she entered Penn Station, she found the nearest restroom and went inside a stall. Pris knew that ultimately, she had been spared; just as they had gotten to Roy, they could have easily gotten to her during the foolish pursuit of the truck. However, that didn't automatically mean that she would be safe from harm indefinitely; circumstances change, and therefore, courses of action change as well. *They* may opt to take a different path at an instant's notice.

She took out her morphing unit from the backpack, which a *Homo sapiens* would have taken for a smartphone on steroids given its current configuration that Pris had defined, and reconfigured it to serve as a scanner. A few seconds later, the analysis was complete: there was a quantum emitter attached to the bottom of her shoe, probably placed there while she had been inside the truck. She could now confirm that at least one extraterrestrial being was behind it all, for this technology was beyond anything that could possibly be created by Earth's twenty-first century civilization. If there was ever any doubt, it had been instantly vaporized.

Pris reconfigured the morphing unit so that she could use it to remove the grain-sized emitter. Holding it with her right hand, a thin blade-like element noiselessly protruded from its front side, and gently guided her hand towards the precise location of the emitter. Once the tip of the blade came into contact with it, three prongs took hold of it, allowing Pris to dislodge it from the sole of her shoe.

With the emitter now inside the morphing unit, Pris was able to analyze it. The morphing unit was able to create an exact replica and activate it the instant the original emitter was deactivated. It was a seamless transition, impossible to detect by whoever was receiving the signal, given the particular configuration of this emitter, and the technology we were able to use to counter it.

Pris left the stall, washed her hands as would be expected of her −not wanting to attract any unnecessary attention to herself by not doing so−and walked towards the large departure board located in the station's main concourse.

She identified the first train that would be leaving the station (Amtrak's 2171 Acela Express headed to Washington on track number two), and knowing that she only had three minutes left, half-walked, half-ran, so as to get there on time. She played the part of the I-don't-want-to-be-late-and-miss-my-train commuter perfectly, blending in with the hundreds of *Homo sapiens* that were moving to and fro inside the station, sidestepping the seemingly-endless stream of tourists that permanently dotted Grand Central Terminal.

She went halfway down the platform, stepped inside the train, located the first seat that happened to be available, and sat down, placing the backpack on her lap.

Pris scanned the area and did not detect anything out of the ordinary. Then a man in a business suit sans the tie (probably having ripped it off now that his work day was over), who was sitting on the other side of the aisle, smiled at her as she inadvertently made eye contact with him; she simply nodded and looked away, not worrying about this exchange, since she knew perfectly well that *Homo sapiens* males flirted *innocently?* every chance they got.

Pris noticed without looking directly at the businessman that he now had his eyes closed, probably trying to take a nap (Pris' eye structure was capable of focusing on anything within view without having to stare directly at the point of interest, another of the many structural and functional differences of Pris' design as compared to that of the *Homo sapiens* which she emulated only outwardly and chemically-structurally).

Pris immediately took out the morphing unit and inconspicuously began to attach the emitter she had replicated onto the cushion underneath her seat.

As she was doing this, a dullish-sounding female voice announced over the PA the following: "This will be the final call on Amtrak's Acela Express Train 2171 en route to Washington departing at 12:27 p.m., making no station stops in between. This will be the final call on Amtrak's Acela Express Train 2171 to Washington departing at 12:27 p.m. All aboard." Pris had been able to finish just in time.

She nudged the businessman to get his attention. "Excuse me, I'm sorry to trouble you, but is this really headed to Washington?" Pris was already out of her seat, hardly waiting for the confirmation.

"Yes... wrong train?" the businessman asked.

"Yes! That was close! Thank you!"

Pris left quickly, without waiting for the man to answer back, and was able to exit the train just as the doors began to close.

Pris knew that this ruse would not buy her much time—if even an instant at all—but anything was better than nothing, even *the possibility of something* is better than *the guarantee of nothing*. She used the 8th Avenue exit, and once outside turned right towards Columbus Circle, in front of Central Park. From there, turning right, a short five-block walk around the park's perimeter would take her to The Pierre hotel. She would get a room and plan her next steps from there (had she not been traveling incognito, she would have already made the reservations and paid for the room).

Still unwilling to emit even the faintest of extraterrestrial signals,

Pris remained out of touch from the metanet and thus from spaceship me. She felt like a speck of dust blowing in stormy winds, and that *others* were in full control of the currents...

10. My Other Selves

Pris was not the only one trying to remain incognito. With Manhattan Roy out of action, there were now ninety-eight other versions of myself roaming Earth, from sea to tempestuous sea, from polar ice cap to polar ice cap. That's figuratively speaking, of course, for all of my other selves were in fact deployed in major cities. Save for the occasional isolated trip that they would have to make into remote regions of the planet, when the design of the mission so determined it, and which occurred mainly to accomplish the scientific goals of this quest, like collecting samples–of biological origin or otherwise, or obtaining field measurements, for example–they mostly spent their days in heavily populated areas.

It should not come as a surprise that although they were all replicas of myself (well, of a particular *variant* of my original self, for the physical characteristics have a strong say in personality), they were all simultaneously unique. Even though their internal computational structures were identical, the instant they became independent beings, moving about, individually exploring, experiencing, and computing, subjected to both external and internal forces and to their resulting vectors, their personalities branched off in different directions. Not uncontrollably so, for there were safeguards built into the computational components designed to prevent such an undesired condition from ever occurring, but enough to be self-evident, obvious. Then there was the aspect of their external differences: as if occupying distinct space-time positions was not enough, those physiognomical variations elicited unique responses from the *Homo sapiens* crowd, which in turn made them even more unique.

What follows now is a chronologically accurate, spliced set of events that were either reported to spaceship-bound me as they occurred, or at a later time after they happened having been stored momentarily in ad-hoc temporary structures. I have taken a few minor liberties to fill in the gaps of these recreations, knowing the subjects as well as I do (what an understatement!), along with their individual quirks. Nothing that would make the events unreliable, however. Most of these events, by the way, took place simultaneously as Manhattan Roy was attacked and effectively destroyed.

Paris Roy was having coffee at a local *boulangerie-patisserie*, enjoying the cool, cloudy afternoon weather the city was experiencing. He was sitting at a table, right on the sidewalk, reading the previous day's edition of *Le Monde*, since he had been unable to get to it until then, for reasons that are not really important.

He was, of course, online at that point, since none of us had any idea of what was about to transpire. When he detected the corrupt quantum signal, he knew Manhattan Roy had been terminated.

Paris Roy scanned the area immediately−dedicating most of his computational resources to the task−to determine if he was also in danger. Nothing seemed out of the ordinary.

In the distance, the distinct sound of a *Police Nationale* vehicle in action could be heard, and based on the increasing frequency, approaching towards his general location. Nothing terribly uncommon, but enough so to put him on edge.

He called out "Monsieur!" and signaled for the check, taking out his wallet, knowing perfectly well that he owed exactly six euros.

The siren was approaching rapidly, and before the waiter came back with the check, Paris Roy saw the white Renault Mégane III with the characteristic blue and red colored designs turn a sharp corner, the tires capriciously complaining by blowing out smoke and generating a screeching noise, accelerate the block that stood between them, and come to an abrupt halt exactly in front of where he happened to be sitting, inches away from hitting a signpost.

The two *policiers* got off the vehicle, ran towards him pointing their guns, and yelled for him to raise his arms and to slowly stand up and to move away from the table, *immédiatement!*

Paris Roy tried to scan their brains, to see if he could buy himself some time by immobilizing them, using bursts of electromagnetic waves, but he couldn't get a reading. That was not expected.

Paris Roy did raise his arms, knowing that to fight would be futile since he was not in possession of any weapon whatsoever, and stood up. One of the *policiers* rushed behind him, grabbed him by the wrists, lowered his arms and handcuffed him.

Paris Roy was forced inside the vehicle, where a third being waited.

One of the patrons that witnessed the whole thing, however unreliable her memory may be, being a *Homo sapiens*, would later report that the suspect seemed to have fallen asleep the instant he was placed inside the vehicle; that had been the moment Paris Roy had been deactivated.

Just as with Manhattan Roy, Paris Roy's final quantum data transmission had also become corrupted seconds before the complete shut-down had taken place.

Considering the fact that we never heard from him again, it was obvious to conclude that he had joined Manhattan Roy in the *by then* rapidly growing list of the earthly deactivated versions of myself.

The two *policiers* were thus probably extraterrestrials, and had been in possession of shields that prevented Roy from scanning them and immobilizing them. Furthermore, they had chosen not to simply deactivate Paris Roy where he had been sitting, leaving him behind for the real Police Nationale to take him away; that clearly meant that they wanted to have possession of the body so as to analyze its *extraterrestrial qualities* as well. Or perhaps they had another agenda instead.

At this point in the story, eighty-seven Roys were still active on Earth. Although that number would quickly dwindle.

The last thing we knew of Los Angeles Roy, for example, was that she was swimming in the ocean in Newport Beach, California, about three hundred yards from the Newport Pier (yes, *she*; forty-nine of my Earth-bound versions emulated the *Homo sapiens* female). Nobody witnessed a thing, not surprisingly, since she had been by herself. Her deactivation had been swift and probably perpetrated from under the water; pulling the body away after deactivating the neuronal system would have been simple to accomplish discreetly.

Vancouver Roy had been alpine hiking on Whistler mountain, about eighty miles north of the city. He had joined a group of seventeen like-minded individuals, but had apparently lost his footing near a cliff, having gone too close for the comfort of others. What they did not know was that he had been swooshed off the mountain by extraterrestrials. Of course, the body was never found.

Moscow Roy was driving down the infamous MKAD (Moskovskaya Koltsevaya Avtomobilnaya Doroga, or the Moscow Ring Automobile Highway), on the southern part of Moscow, closing in on the Varshavskoye and Simferopolskoye freeways. The local time was 7:20 pm. An eighty year old man named Nikolai was seated next to her, wanting anxiously to get home safely.

Nikolai had accidentally spilled coffee on Moscow Roy's sweater, while sitting outside the Neskuchny Garden, the oldest park in the city, watching the Moscow River. After the incident, they chatted for a while, and when Moscow Roy found out that the old man lived all the way down in Shcherbinka, a borough about 20 miles south of where they were, and relied on the public transportation system to get back home, she offered to give him a ride.

Nikolai was regretting the decision to accept the offer. Traffic was (unfortunately for him) light, which meant that a considerable number of drivers were free to test how fast their cars could go, something they seldom got to do. To make matters worse for Nikolai's heart as well as his blood pressure, the infamous potholes that were strewn about and the light rain that had started coming down only a few minutes ago made it a truly horrible experience for him.

Moscow Roy noticed Nikolai's reaction, of course, and slowed down, as much as was safe to do so, while she tried to calm down the old man without actually point out his nervousness, realizing too late that this ride-offering had probably been a mistake. They were very near their next exit, however, and from there, the Varshavskoye freeway would take them straight to Nikolai's old neighborhood. Only ten more minutes, tops.

Up ahead, they were about to cross the railway tracks that ran under the MKAD, riding, of course, the road's overpass.

Moscow Roy turned to look at Nikolai; he seemed a bit calmer now, probably because he knew the trip was almost over.

It was at that moment when a black SUV swerved all the way from the left-most lane and hit them in the front side of their vehicle. Moscow Roy tried to control the car, and was in fact able to avoid crashing against the guardrail. Her extraterrestrial processing structures were the only reason why she had been successful.

Their car's momentum had now changed, and was sending them barreling towards the center lane. Moscow Roy stepped on the gas pedal all the way, while turning the steering wheel in order to ensure that the front tires aligned themselves to the momentum's direction vector. She noticed that Nikolai had his eyes closed, and was mumbling unintelligibly. She hoped that the old man's heart was healthy enough to survive the scare.

What Moscow Roy didn't know was that a white Chevrolet Niva had been following behind them four miles back, and just as Moscow Roy had managed to control the car and avoid the guardrail, the white sedan accelerated and hit them on the same side that the black SUV had hit them on only two seconds before.

This time, the front left tire was unable to take the impact and it blew out as soon as the pressure crossed the critical threshold. The force of the crash sent them towards the guardrail once again, and with one tire gone, Moscow Roy couldn't control the vehicle anymore. Extraterrestrial powers included.

They hit the guardrail almost head-on, which was not sturdy enough to stop them from flying off the MKAD, not at that angle of impact, leaping off the road, and instants later crashing down into a set of railway tracks that lay below the road –perpendicularly–twenty feet below the MKAD.

Nikolai's heart stopped beating the instant the car came into contact with the rail tracks; Moscow Roy, on the other hand, was still operational. She turned her head and saw Nikolai's frozen expression of fear on his face, and knew the old man couldn't be helped. Moscow Roy also knew that she had to escape from the attackers as soon as she had a chance.

A burst of high energy particles, centered on the car's gas tank, was all it took to explosively deactivate Moscow Roy, instantly…

An extraterrestrial had been driving a blue AvtoVAZ Lada Granta, one of the most popular modern cars in Russia, following the white Niva close behind, and had fired off the explosive burst once Moscow Roy's car had jumped off the guard rail.

When the Muscovite Police arrived on the scene, they figured it had been just another casualty in the long list of fatal accidents that occurred almost daily on the MKAD, based on their report that I later accessed.

They found charred shreds of glass belonging to a Garant vodka bottle inside the mangled car, which led them to believe that the driver had been drinking as well. The bottle, of course, had been planted there beforehand.

Even though the explosion and the ensuing fire had practically disintegrated most of the victims' bodies, sufficient pieces of burnt bone and teeth remained so that the police officers could correctly report the number of victims, though not their gender, and certainly not their identities. As for an autopsy, that would be completely out of the question.

And on that day, on and on and on... Different set ups, different actors, different backgrounds, same results.

By the time the blitzkrieg was over, on July 19th, 2007, ninety-eight of my Earth-bound selves had been unwillingly, purposefully, and untimely deactivated. Nikolai had not been the only *Homo sapiens* casualty either, although he had the distinction of being the oldest victim of the lot. Twenty-five others (four women and seven men, ranging in age from thirty-four to seventy-seven) had been murdered, all innocent people who had been unlucky enough to have attracted the attention of eight Roys that day, or that had simply been in the wrong place at the wrong time during the deliberate attacks. The collateral material damage included one derailed train, a sunken boat, eight totaled vehicles, a collapsed pedestrian bridge, two structures burned to the ground, and a section of a sidewalk engulfed by what the local authorities incorrectly assumed to have been the work of a sinkhole.

Because these events did not take place in a single city (or continent, for that matter), nobody outside of our small circle of extraterrestrials could really make the connection.

There was one last remaining Roy; he was in the city of Oaxaca, Mexico, when the avalanche of attacks began. In hindsight, I can correctly assert that one of the city's worst thunderstorms in its recent history was what had foiled the extraterrestrial's effort to deactivate him.

11. Monte Albán, Oaxaca

Oaxaca Roy had decided to visit the world-famous archeological site of Monte Albán, located in the municipality of Santa Cruz Xoxocotlán, just twenty minutes away from the city's Zócalo, or central square. It served purposes on multiple levels.

He was renting in the city of Oaxaca, located in the state of the same name, in the country of México, a surprisingly large room in an old colonial *casona*, or house, with the characteristic high ceilings that were in vogue at the time of its construction, which helped keep interiors cool. Located two blocks away from the city's central square, it gave him direct access to the city's heart and soul, an often frequented area not only by the tourists, but also by the locals of every socioeconomic background.

Roy knew the weather would not be great that day, but he didn't mind the rain, and in fact, welcomed it.

Just a few minutes before the attacks began, he had been walking around the *Patio Hundido* (or submerged patio), a rectangular-shaped section of the structural complex that rests on top of Monte Albán, carved fifteen and a half feet deep from the main terrain. He had been walking towards a structure that adorns its center, an *Adoratorio*: a hollow square pyramid, five foot tall, with forty foot sides.

Rain had been falling uninterruptedly for over an hour now, so naturally, Roy was completely drenched.

Lightning strikes could be seen in the distance; its accompanying thunder following close behind, only three to five seconds later, which meant that they were rapidly approaching this ancient site.

Many tourists had left the site seeking shelter down below, fearing the lightning strikes more than the rain itself. Roy, however, knew that given the electromagnetic conditions in their immediate area, there was nothing they needed to fear, at least not yet anyway.

An European-looking tourist that seemed to be in her thirties was leaning against one of the column bases that are located atop the Patio Hundido's perimeter. She was sporting a wide tan-colored hat which offered her some protection against the rain (at least as far as her face was concerned) and was seemingly waiting for someone. She was, in fact, humming a song.

Oaxaca Roy focused his attention on her because while a particular loud thunder had startled the few tourists still braving the elements, she had remained unfazed. Roy calculated those odds and found them to be extremely low. She could be deaf, of course, but based on other cues he was now recalling and reviewing, that didn't seem to be the case here.

At 10:20 a.m., when the attacks began everywhere against all of my Roy-selves on Earth, the woman, on cue, turned halfway towards him. The instant that she directed a wave of high-energy particles towards Roy's midbrain, which were meant to deactivate him on the spot, the improbable happened.

Lightning struck the corner of the Adoratorio, which stood partly in the way between Roy and the extraterrestrial, absorbing and diverting away the bulk of the particles from Oaxaca Roy, saving him from instant cessation.

He did notice the attack, of course, because a few particles managed to make it through, insignificantly damaging several brain cells. These particles were sufficient in number to trigger his sensors, and based on a quick analysis, he was able to figure out where exactly they had come from.

Instantly, Oaxaca Roy sprang into action. He dived to the ground, seeking the protection of the Adoratorio's five foot wall, removing his morphing unit from the belt pouch that was wrapped around his waist, as he rolled to a full stop. He pressed himself hard against the wet rock.

He instructed the morphing unit to reconfigure itself as a space-time shield, activating it as soon as it was ready, just three seconds later.

If any *Homo sapiens* had been there to witness it, they would have seen raindrops suddenly begin to bounce off an invisible structure surrounding Roy's body, which seemed to almost touch the ground, as if he was wearing an invisible, waterproof cloak. Roy stood up, and knowing he didn't have a lot of time since the energy requirements of this particular shield design were extremely high (quickly draining the morphing unit's power), he ran towards his attacker.

The extraterrestrial that had been trying to pass off as a western European tourist had been caught completely off guard by the seemingly impossible turn of events, but seamlessly came up with an alternate plan.

She ran down the narrow steps, impossibly fast, and headed straight for Roy, ready to fire another blast of high-energy particles. Surely lightning would not strike twice in the same spot.

As she approached the central structure, she saw Roy rising above the wall, and must have realized that he had activated a shield, because she froze and dove to the ground herself.

Oaxaca Roy didn't know what to expect; even though he was receiving reports of the attacks that were simultaneously taking place elsewhere, and thus figured correctly that this was part of a massive worldwide operation, he had no way of knowing who was behind it, nor what type of weapons they may possess. It was conceivable that a more powerful attack could target him from anywhere, and there would be nothing he could do to stop that.

He decided, of course, to guide his actions based on the probability that they would be successful, and to prepare for what he could conceivably defend himself against, as opposed to considering scenarios that there was nothing he could really do anything about. The latter was a pointless exercise, while the former at least offered him the potential of success.

He deployed all ten miniature robots that he had with him, sending them to the other side of the Adoratorio: nine to go around from his right, onto go around from his left.

As soon as the robots reached the corner with the side where the extraterrestrial lay, they jumped off into her view, firing a short yet dense burst of positively-charged ions which they had been able to channel from the surrounding area. Each robot took its turn, one by one, in half-a-second intervals.

Roy, meanwhile, climbed over the wall and into the Adoratorio's hollow center, and crawled his way towards the opposite end of the wall, where his attacker lay, in wait, on the other side.

The lone robot that had been waiting to the left of where the extraterrestrial was hiding, on Roy's cue raced towards Roy's attacker and sacrificed itself by serving to bridge the minuscule gap that separated the extraterrestrial and the wet ground.

Roy, ready for this moment, jumped towards the extraterrestrial, and upon touching her, caused an increase in the strength of the localized electric field. This in turn meant that the extraterrestrial's corona discharge exceeded a critical threshold, giving way to an upward streamer.

The lightning strike paralyzed the extraterrestrial long enough for Roy to deactivate his attacker... Roy's shield had made him completely immune to the tremendous flow of electricity that had taken place only instants before.

He wanted to keep the body, for numerous reasons. He could see that nobody had been a witness to any of this, but that would not last long. Although it was still raining, and hard, it would probably stop in less than thirty minutes.

He carried the body to the northwest corner of the Patio Hundido, which was located on the edge of the mountain. Oaxaca Roy then climbed up the stairs with the limp extraterrestrial body in his arms, and hid behind a tall L-shaped wall and a large tree that offered shelter from any prying eyes from down below.

Roy activated the shield around both of them, drastically reducing its intensity since all he wanted was to keep the water from interfering with his activities, and scanned the whole body for later analysis. He was particularly interested in the extraterrestrial's computational structure.

Once he had the data he needed, he deactivated the shield, allowing water to once again bathe the area. He took several samples of tissue using two of his miniature robots, and then reconfigured the morphing unit so that it could be used to produce a dense plasma field.

The intense–almost invisible–localized film of ionized gas taken from the surrounding atmosphere quickly and efficiently evaporated close to ninety-nine percent of the matter that made up the deactivated extraterrestrial's body–including the clothes and accessories she'd been wearing–the steam by-product dissipating quickly as the raindrops effectively drenched it out. All remaining ashes fell to the ground, and were completely absorbed and carried away by the rain that was coming down even more intensely now, forming thick rivulets all around Oaxaca Roy. Had the ancient Zapotecs that built this Monte Albán site had been a witness to these events, they would have –without a doubt–mistaken Oaxaca Roy for one of their many gods.

Roy climbed back down into the Patio Hundido, and scanned the area to make sure that the extraterrestrial had not left anything behind that could spur the curiosity of the authorities, or of the tourists once they returned.

He did detect a single *foreign* object. He walked towards the southwest corner where it lay, and used his morphing unit, trying to determine what it was.

Made of a soft, gel-like substance, porous enough to allow gas molecules to freely flow in and out of its hollow interior, it housed living bacteria, triads of them contained within minute balloon-like structures that numbered in the millions. Oaxaca Roy pocketed the find after determining that it was safe to handle it.

After picking up several pieces of clothing that had shredded off during the lightning event, Oaxaca Roy decided there was nothing else that he needed to clear away from the scene. He was now ready to leave.

As he turned towards the southern side of the submerged Patio Hundido, a man appeared into view, rapidly climbing down the stairs, clearly headed towards him. The forty-something man, donning blue jeans and a vinyl rain jacket that covered him from the top of his head to the bottom of his ankles (in addition to topping off the outfit with a light brown waterproof safari hat), was yelling something at the top of bis lungs, impossible to understand given the weather conditions and the distance that separated them.

Oaxaca Roy was finally able to know what was being said to him as they approached each other and got closer. The *Homo sapiens* was speaking in very proficient English, though with a clearly local accent.

"You need to get away from here, quick! Let's go! Did you see her Señor? A tourist, European, red jacket? No? Come on! There is lighting coming down here! We need to go back!," gasping for breath, agitated, and sounding desperate to leave.

"No, I did not see anyone! Should we look for her?" Oaxaca Roy asked, trying to sound surprised, scared, anxious, the expected reaction under the circumstances.

"No! Too dangerous! I hope she is in one of the tunnels! Vámonos, ándale!" The man was running fast now, assuming the *clueless turista* was following closely behind, not turning to check. They climbed up the stairs, and headed to the mountain site's exit, on the eastern side, running non-stop down the slippery trail that led to the on-site museum, one more group desperately anxious to use it as a shelter.

Oaxaca Roy later found out that the *female tourist* had paid that specific individual to be her guide for the day, and that half an hour before she had attacked Roy, she had asked the guide to wait for her inside the Nissan Tsuru taxicab that the man used as his primary source of income.

They never did find her, and although the local authorities searched the site, including all sides of the mountain, they simply gave up and concluded that she had probably left Monte Albán on her own, probably after hooking up with another tourist. Not an impossible scenario at all.

The fact that nobody reported her missing in the days that followed meant that the case was closed for good.

12. On the move

After an uneventful set of flights, on Sunday, July 22nd, Oaxaca Roy became Manhattan Roy. He had changed genders and his overall physiognomy three times, once for each of the flights he had boarded between that day and the previous one. Roy had flown from Oaxaca to Mexico City, ridden a bus to Toluca, flown nonstop to Miami, where he rented a car and had driven to Palm Beach International Airport; after spending the night at the airport's Hilton, he completed the last leg of his journey by flying into LaGuardia International Airport in the morning.

He was unaware if Pris was still around, and if so, whether or not she had left Manhattan. But starting his search where we had last seen her was the logical choice, because even if she had left the city, he might be able to find a clue as to her whereabouts. Besides, a Roy had been attacked and deactivated here; he would be able to look into this event as well.

What Manhattan Roy–whom I would have labeled *the second* had the first one survived the attack–now knew beyond any doubt was that he was the last of the Earth-bound Roys still in operation. Therefore, the need for me to specify which Roy I am talking about from this moment on has vanished.

Just as Pris had stopped communicating with me directly via the metanet to avoid being detected, Roy had followed suit, and so was completely offline as well. He headed straight to The Pierre, of course, which is not, by any means, a coincidence at all. While true that Pris had headed to the same hotel the previous day, there is a very simple explanation for this.

Every city on Earth is assigned a quantum probability matrix, with values defined specifically for the duration of the mission, which allows for, among other things—and there are many, believe me—the selection of a hotel should the need arise, incommunicado or not (that discrete variable, for example, forms part of the overall quantum algorithm).

At this moment in time, my spaceship-bound self was out of the loop, completely. I had no idea where Pris was, or even if she was still operational. I did not know where Oaxaca Roy was, or if he was still operational. And although I had access to the same quantum algorithms that they had access to, and could thus *potentially* compute what they could compute, without knowing where they were, I couldn't produce any useful outputs.

Even if I could initiate a data-sharing transmission, protocol required that I wait to be contacted, not the other way around, since while I may be up here in the comfort and safety of space, they are millions of miles away, on the surface of an alien planet, with alien beings, and in the current circumstances, with extraterrestrials trying to destroy them to boot.

Roy eventually found himself outside of The Pierre hotel, on the corner of 5th Avenue and E 61st Street. He was greeted by a white-gloved bellhop named Sam, fully suited in the traditional garb, who after confirming with him that he would be a guest of the hotel, promptly took his carry-on and accompanied him across the checkerboard sidewalk floor to the main entrance. There, a white-gloved doorman named Tom welcomed him —smiling—as he pushed the revolving door for him, only to lead him to the front desk once Roy found himself inside.

The lobby was clearly meant to be luxurious, highly ornate and detailed, but not pretentious. The black, white, and gold checkered marble floor clearly caught the attention of the visual field of anyone that happened to walk in. After checking in, a different bellhop took him to one of the guest elevators, where a short, white-gloved attendant named Sasha pushed the button for him. Upon reaching the twelfth floor, Sam led him to his room where his carry-on bag was already waiting for him, having been delivered by another−also white-gloved?−bellhop, using a separate service elevator. Roy was given the grand tour of the three hundred square foot room−even though it had only two distinct spaces: the bedroom and the bathroom−and received a detailed explanation of how to turn lights on and off, control the temperature, and operate the seemingly complicated TV system, which was currently displaying the time, date, local temperature, and the name that Roy had used to get the room. After being tipped a twenty dollar bill, the bellhop left promptly and silently, closing the door behind him.

Roy was careful to do everything that would be expected of a guest that was supposed to be staying in town for three weeks, having been unexpectedly diverted to Manhattan on business from what had originally been just a two day trip to Miami (that is the cover story that Roy had decided to tell the somewhat surprised front-desk receptionist in order to justify the fact that he had not made a reservation, was in possession of only a light carry-on bag and a backpack, and would probably be staying for two weeks−barring any other twists and turns of his foreseeable future. Roy knew that it was best to have a credible story of who he was and what he was doing here, especially while staying at a hotel. Too many prying eyes that could not really be avoided.

He unpacked his few belongings, set the toiletries where they were normally placed, bagged a couple of previously worn clothes so the hotel could take care of them, hung two shirts and a light jacket in the closet, stocked a single drawer with what was left without filling it, and headed downstairs, taking only his backpack with him.

He headed to the hotel's 2E Lounge to seek for *the* sign of Pris' presence. Located off the main lobby, as he walked down the short flight of stairs that led to its entrance, Roy could see the dark gold-colored bar, and two long and narrow black vases that contained overflowing plants, which adorned the sides of the well-stocked golden-colored shelves.

The layout was clean, elegant, a bit eclectic, in keeping with the style of all public areas of the hotel. Upon entering the lounge proper, he saw the round, short tables that were arranged in a criss-cross pattern on either side of the aisle, all tables seating four, with matching dark-golden, black-framed low chairs. The place was empty save for one partially-occupied table: two women were seated in a corner, tropical-looking drinks in hand, and apparently oblivious to Roy's muted entrance.

Roy wondered if the people working this section of the hotel would be wearing white gloves as well, but figured that to be unlikely. How could they efficiently and safely prepare the paraphernalia of food and beverage items offered here, as well as handle the tableware, if they did? He was right, of course. The suited bartender, a man who turned out to be from New Delhi, greeted him promptly, bare hands in plain view of all. Roy wondered if this would be cause for alarm amongst the rest of the hotel employees, or if it would define a caste system of sorts, one that overruled the more common one that is typically found in *Homo sapiens* organizations such as these.

"Welcome to the 2E Lounge, sir," Roy was welcomed, with a beaming smile.

A waiter donning dress pants and shirt, tie, and vest, but not the suit's jacket, offered him a table on the opposite side of where the women were seated, perhaps neurotically aiming to balance the amount of organic material that would be currently occupying the low-lit room.

"Good afternoon, Sir. I am Louis. Will you be having lunch with us today, sir?"

"No Louis, thank you. I'd just like to have some tea."

"Excellent, sir. Allow me to bring you our fine selection," the waiter said, and promptly, as well as silently, left to accommodate the patron's wishes.

Roy scanned the room and almost instantly identified what he was looking for. The lounge contained four thick columns symmetrically distributed on either side, painted black, Corinthian style.

Fortunately, all the tables closest to the columns were unoccupied, although he only cared about one in particular: the one specified by the quantum matrix guide which he had been using to make every single one of his decisions so far. Given the city where Pris had last been seen, it singled out the hotel in this city–and relevant for now–where to look for a message from Pris if she was still in the city and had in fact come to this hotel.

If he did not find anything, he would leave a message for Pris should she come looking for him at a later date, and simply continue to follow the quantum matrix guide (the *QMG*?).

The waiter returned with a long list of teas that the hotel was able (and willing) to offer. Just as he was about to hand it to him, Roy spoke to him first.

"I'm sorry to trouble you Louis, but would you mind if I changed tables?" Roy stood up as he asked this.

"Please... but of course, sir." The waiter did not question the reason, wanting to accommodate the patron's wishes, *ipso facto*. Biomass balance be damned?

Roy walked over to the table that was closest to the third column, as counted from the southwestern-most position in the room (ties would have been settled by the matrix using a bearing of true north instead of the local, magnetic north). He sat down, not really caring about the arrangement of the tables themselves at all, nor about the particular table he was sitting in either, but rather focusing on the specific column that stood in front of him.

"Ah. This is perfect, Louis. Thank you," Roy said as he sat down, took the tea menu from the waiter and looked at the herbal offerings being currently offered.

"You are most welcome, sir." Louis responded.

"I'll have the Pierre blend, Louis. Good choice, you think?"

"Certainly, sir. It happens to be my favorite," the waiter answered, perhaps truthfully.

"Would you care for a sampling of sandwiches or pastries, sir?"

Roy thought about that and decided to skip it. The waiter promptly and quietly left, taking the tea menu with him.

Being forced to go incognito meant that he could not produce any kind of emissions that are not normally produced by *Homo sapiens*, or else he could risk being detected. Therefore, Roy had been forced not only to go offline, but also to shut down many of his internal computational structures, for even though they were ultimately comprised of neuronal networks (with distinct properties), all organic-carbon based, utilizing metabolic processes that are normally–and for the most part–present in *Homo sapiens*, some of them do produce measurable emissions that are not normal to the species, and therefore, extraterrestrials could easily detect them. This greatly limited Roy's ability to compute, though not to the point of reducing him to that of the *Homo sapiens'* level, the species he was currently emulating; there were other processes that enhanced his perception and computational abilities without producing any abnormal emissions that Roy could still use.

What Roy truly lamented was the fact that operating in this reduced computational state greatly limited the type of sensory information that he could have access to. He could deal with the slowness, but he missed many of his multidimensional perception capabilities.

As protocol required, Roy took out his morphing unit, which was currently set to emulate a rather bulky version of the Motorola Q9h smartphone, a model that was available commercially for the first time that year. Although a very limited phone compared to what became available only a few years later, it did have a digital camera, which is the only thing that Roy needed to determine if Pris had left him a message here in Manhattan.

He took a picture of the column from the appropriate angle, the special light from the flash illuminating it briefly.

Satisfied with the picture, Roy used his fingers (couldn't use neuronal waves like he normally did) to access the appropriate application stored in the morphing unit. Using spectrum analysis, filtering out specific visible light frequencies also determined by the quantum matrix guide, he found what he was looking for.

A set of three symbols were clearly visible on the morphing unit's screen. Roy now knew that Pris had in fact headed to the hotel after going offline yesterday afternoon, knew the room number she was staying in, and knew that she had checked in on the previous day. The symbols also specified three specific ratio values involving her facial features, which would help Roy to identify her regardless of how she configured the rest of her physiognomy, or what gender Pris used to appear of *Homo sapiens* origin.

He decided it was too risky to just show up to her room and knock on the door, for they were on different floors. With all the gloved people working every square foot of the place (never mind the hundreds of security cameras that recorded almost every cubic inch of public space within the hotel's property as well), Roy was forced to be extra careful. He thought about the matrix's programming, and figured they could have done a better job of location choice (a hotel with less service personnel would have been nice—a lot less intrusive). Nothing is ever perfect.

He ruled out both of the women that were still chatting away the time, since none of the three facial ratios matched. Pris was not one of them. He needed to share with her what he had found out about the extraterrestrials that were behind the mutations and the attacks, based on the samples he took in Monte Albán.

"Your tea, sir." Louis served him the hot beverage from a glass pot, steam still coming out from the sides of the crown and from the spout as the golden liquid filled the all-white porcelain cup, gently lowering the now only partially-full pot on the table before leaving.

Roy sipped the tea carefully, finding it very insipid since his senses were extremely limited, and thus losing the added dimensions that greatly enhanced the typical *Homo sapiens* food tasting experience. Trivial matters, though, compared to what was at stake.

As he pondered his next move, he heard the sound of footsteps coming from the lounge's entrance.

He instantly knew it was Pris. The three ratios were a match. He waited for her to make the next move, not knowing how she wanted to play this. After all, he had to conclude that because she already had a room at The Pierre, and he did not know what her cover story had been when she checked in (perhaps without a reservation as well), that it was best to allow her to take the lead. He was not aware of large swaths of data contained in the QMG, something that was a matter of design, and not accidental.

On the other hand, Roy knew that Pris did not know what *his* cover story had been either...

Without saying a word, Pris looked into Roy's eyes and quickly conveyed the information that was needed, using a series of subtle eye movements that were completely undetectable to the *Homo sapiens* eye. Likewise, Roy conveyed what Pris needed to know. The exchange took less than one second, taking place even as Pris approached Roy's table.

"Well finally, you made it! I was worried the company was going to abandon me and that I was going to have to deal with this issue all by myself!" Pris said as soon as she was able to come up with a reasonable story that would justify their knowing each other.

Roy instantly stood up, knowing he would be expected to do so. "Hi! I didn't know that you were already here... They should have told me! Well, I guess it slipped their mind. Please, sit down, have some tea with me, if you like."

They gave each other a warm hug, and kissed briefly on the lips, like two *friends?* might do. He pulled away a chair for her to sit in, right next to his.

Given their limited communication capabilities, they relied on the tiny twitches and eye movements that were impossible to be seen by the *Homo sapiens* eye.

She ordered a tea for herself (organic peppermint, her favorite), and afterwards they whispered *literally nothing* into their ears (simply trying to convey the idea of the *type* of relationship they shared), asked for the check, and left together, holding hands.

They had decided to head outside and walk in Central Park, where they felt safer exchanging what they both had been through since going offline, the moment the global attacks had begun against our mission. That, and to share what they had been able to find out so far regarding the identity of the extraterrestrials.

Out on the sidewalk, they headed left towards the corner of 5th Avenue. They waited for the walk sign to give them the right-of-way, crossed 5th Avenue, and walked straight into the park. Roy and Pris walked through East Drive, and ended in front of The Pond, one of the many artificial lakes that dot the public property, this one situated on the southeast corner of the most famous park in New York.

They sat down on one of the many benches that line the inner walking tracks, facing the water. They were alone for the most part, though others did walk by in front of them, some taking the usual Sunday stroll, others power walking or jogging. There were a few people occupying nearby benches, but nothing that stood out to them as being out of the ordinary.

Pris and Roy continued to communicate on two different levels: using speech, they did not diverge from their story, that of two high-level employees who were in the city to follow up on a deal worth millions to the company they worked for, although they also happened to be more than co-workers, more than friends. That conversation, however, was worthless to them, a script devoid of useable data.

At another level, they were using the same minute eye movements and facial twitches that they had used in the lounge, which allowed them to convey much more than they could have done using speech. It encoded a far richer symbolic system than any of the *Homo sapiens* spoken word systems did. Although they could have mounted the same information on the sound waves coming out of their larynxes by modulating the amplitude, frequency, or both, they had decided to skip that option because the process involved generating a type of emission clearly not of *Homo sapiens* origin, one that could easily be detected by the extraterrestrials, if not by the *Homo sapiens* themselves.

Had anyone overheard Roy and Pris talking, they would have thought nothing of it. They were practically indistinguishable from the people around them, regardless of the technology used to try to observe them with. Barring, of course, extraterrestrial technology; they could easily detect the voluntary eye movement and know that it served to encode meaning. But they would have to be able to monitor the movement directly. Pris and Roy were not producing any alien emissions whatsoever.

After Pris updated Roy on everything she had been through since the attacks had begun, Roy began to tell her about his experience.

Pris promptly realized that Oaxaca Roy should have been deactivated on the day of the attacks... That it was only as a result of a highly unlikely chain of events that he was still around to tell the story.

As to the samples Roy had obtained, he explained to Pris that back in Oaxaca, before boarding the plane bound for Mexico City (on the first leg of the trip), he had used the morphing unit to analyze them. He had also reviewed the scan of the extraterrestrial's body which he had performed before vaporizing it (he would share with Pris the raw data once they were back at the hotel so Pris could process it as well).

Roy then told her that he knew *unequivocally* who they were dealing with.

The extraterrestrials that had attacked them were, in fact, from the Allegiance.

Pris asked him to clarify…

"The being that attacked me had processing structures that are distinctively of allegiance design and technology. All of the metabolic processes that I was able to pinpoint from the samples I took are exactly like those that power us. These beings have access to our technology, have been using it, and have adapted it to suit their goals," he explained.

"We need to advise spaceship Roy. As soon as we can safely do so," Pris suggested.

"Yes. But we need to find a way to access the metanet without the possibility of being detected. Because if they are as advanced as the Allegiance, they should certainly be able to pick up any quantum signals we use."

"I agree. However, Roy, now we have a huge advantage over them. We know their capabilities—barring any unlikely technological leaps they may have come up with on their own, and therefore, we also happen to know their limitations. This will help us come up with our best course of action."

Roy and Pris continued to exchange data matrices, computational algorithms, logico-analytical structures, and although it took them longer to process it all given the fact that they were operating with drastically reduced capabilities, they eventually came up with a detailed, step-by-step plan that they almost-desperately hoped would work.

They left the park and headed back to the hotel. Because Pris had been upgraded to a suite, they decided to go to her room, the logical choice for two people who might be working on whatever business they had at hand (regardless of what their relationship might be like outside their jobs, which they clearly went out of their way to *inadvertently* advertise for all the hotel employees to see).

They ordered room service; their bodies in desperate need for food in order to continue to function at a heightened metabolic and computational state. While it was delivered, Pris brought up the subject of the USB she had found inside the truck.

"You did not mention it back at the park, Pris. Why not?" It had to be a calculated move on behalf of Pris. Beings like Pris, Roy, us, we do not *forget* things. That *defect?* is the product of an evolutionary-speaking underdeveloped processing system (what you call the brain!). Assuming normal operational conditions, of course.

"It is completely blank. The memory contains nothing but zeros, so it had to have been purposefully cleared. The hardware is typical of these devices... USB 2.0 OTi controller, 8 GB Lexar flash memory chip, equipped with an SKC Shin Chang Electronics 12.000 MHz crystal oscillator. The circuitry design is as average as it gets. The connectors are made with a copper alloy, the casing is plastic, and the shell is stainless steel. Can you imagine using this technology to perform even the most basic of tasks?"

"Impossible... but all civilizations have to begin somewhere, Pris. We are the product of billions of years of collective evolution, progress, localized entropy-reversal. *Homo sapiens* is in its infancy. Now, as to the USB drive, do you still have it?"

"Of course." Pris walked to the table where she had left her backpack, took it out, and threw it across the room to Roy.

He simply held it in his hands, looking at it, unable to perform any relevant scans at the moment, and therefore, not really expecting to discover anything relevant. Pris had already analyzed it, and the possibility that she had missed something was practically nonexistent.

"I thought about the oscillator... perhaps its frequency means something," Pris said.

"Have you checked it?"

"Yes. It is perfectly within range, and yet–" she couldn't finish her sentence. Someone had knocked at her door.

They communicated in silence, all under a second.

Roy: Room service.

Pris: Probably. Too cliché otherwise.

Roy: Funny. But what if it's them?

Pris: It's not. We are safe here. We have not given ourselves away, in any way. Look at the probability matrices.

Roy: The assumption values could be wrong. Look at this one. It gives a different result.

Pris: Matter of perspective. I will be in the bathroom. If anything happens, it will give me enough time to access the metanet and transfer everything we know to date. Spaceship Roy would have to take it from there.

Roy: Go.

"Who is it?" Roy yelled as Pris took out her metanet connector from her backpack and half ran to the bathroom, closing the door behind her. If anything happened to Roy, she would know about it instantly. She would be able to connect to the metanet and download all the data she had collected since the last update she'd executed (just before going incognito at Penn Station the day before).

"Room service," a woman answered from the hallway.

Roy walked to the door, looked through the peephole, and saw a woman dressed in waitress garb with a food cart next to her.

"What is your name, please?" Roy asked, without opening the door.

"Roxana, sir," she replied, seemingly perplexed by the question.

Roy thought about her reaction, and almost opened the door based on that cue alone. But he decided to check with the hotel. He grabbed the phone and pressed the button for room service.

Before anyone answered at the other end of the line, he heard a

-click- coming from the door-lock's mechanism.

Suddenly, the door was pushed wide open.

He saw the woman push the cart into the room, acting normal (whose real name—Roy couldn't help himself from concluding —was probably not Roxana... which was extremely irrelevant, he computed as well).

"Your meal, sir," she was saying as she entered the room.

Roy knew they had been found. He expected to be terminated.

As the door closed behind her, she began to communicate with Roy using quantum waves. Roy was able to process them, even though he was offline and incognito. The waves stimulated his sensors, which Roy activated, considering the circumstances.

Extraterrestrial: Your turn to be terminated. What happened in Monte Albán was extremely unlikely. Nothing like that will save you now. I will not explain why, but just know it is necessary. Your Primary Self may see that, in time—

The transmission was suddenly interrupted.

Roy heard the bathroom door open, and saw Pris come out, holding her morphing unit, which she had configured to emit energy-rays. She had destroyed the woman's processing system completely.

"I had to do it, Roy. If they already know that we are here, using the weapon means nothing. So what if they detect it? They already know where we are."

Roy knew she was right. But why had it been so easy to evade the attack? It did not make any sense.

"Pris, this was too easy. Is this being really an extraterrestrial?"

"Yes. I don't know if the being harmed the real Roxana, which I assume does exist and probably emulated."

"Let's dispose of the being and leave."

They dragged the inert body to the bathroom, lifted it inside the bathtub, turned on the shower, and used the morphing unit to vaporize it. The running water carried away the extraterrestrial's ashes the instant they were produced.

"Do you detect anything, Pris?"

"No. But we better leave now, before they regroup. Assuming that's what they will do, anyway."

Roy and Pris left the hotel carrying with them only their backpacks. Everything else was left back in their rooms. They would never be seen back at The Pierre again—nor would they ever reuse that physiognomy. As far as Earth was concerned, those two had disappeared from the face of the planet for good.

13. The CPU

Pris and Roy had walked away from The Pierre as if nothing had happened. They had later called and asked the front desk to pack their belongings, and to store them away for them, explaining that their business plans had changed unexpectedly and that they were no longer in the city. They promised to get back to them with further instructions.

They had decided to rent a car and to drive to Boston themselves. They had not wanted to take a train or board a plane, for fear that it could put numerous innocent *Homo sapiens* in danger.

In a way, they felt liberated by the experience. Knowing that they had been found even while remaining offline and going incognito, reducing all *un-Homo sapiens* emissions to zero, they figured correctly that it was best to put an end to that. It would be better to maintain all of their abilities at full capacity, and to stay in touch with spaceship me, through the metanet, at all times. At least for the time being. The three of us couldn't make any sense of the extraterrestrial's feeble attempt at terminating Roy and Pris back at the hotel. We were sure they could have proceeded in a much more efficient manner, whereby they would have been actually successful. We did not know what to make of it. Why didn't an army of extraterrestrials attack them? Why were they being allowed to remain functional? The absolute lack of logic was nerving, ridiculous.

It was thus during their drive to Boston that I received an update of all of their data since they had gone offline. I was now in the loop, and would be−in real time. I could help them during their mission, though my principal concern was now to advise the Allegiance. The mission, which had started out as a routine survey, suddenly metamorphosed into a high-level, meta-universal event.

After I had seen from Roy's analysis that someone from the Allegiance was behind the attacks, I had not been surprised at all. The technology they had proven to possess had made that a very real possibility all along.

I prepared and reviewed all of the report matrices that I would be sending to the Allegiance. As soon as they were ready, I contacted the metanet and initiated the transmission. The type of connection I was using allowed me to experience the Allegiance's CPU directly.

Sensory inputs that would otherwise remain turned off came "alive" in me, feeding me data, structures, sensations, experiences, and abilities, in the form of multidimensional quantum matrices, so that I changed *permanently*, evolving, raising my level of consciousness, renewing my design. The experience, however, is not defined by boundaries. The transitions are seamless to the point that I know they happened, but I am unable to sense the specific changes as independent experiences. It is still one continuous, conscious me. I am who I am, regardless of the evolutionary changes I may experience during my active state. The essence changes, and yet I *perceive* it as being the same. Beings with serial-consciousness, as opposed to those that have parallel-consciousness, can never be self-aware of their discrete essences, as they are irreversibly altered in time and instantaneously feel like they had been there all along.

And so during my communication with the CPU, I simultaneously engaged with millions of beings, both physically and virtually, depending on their availability, on myriads of circumstances, and on directives that were sourced from the CPU itself.

Different structures provided different outputs, while challenging the data in unique ways, tweaking it, applying different quantum vectors. Sometimes using physical representations so as to allow us to experience the analysis through the use of *physical* senses (particle-waves, waves, and particles interacting in multidimensional space-time, meshing, clashing, morphing, using the laws of the universe as the ultimate computing machine: the physical laws known or unknown–therein lies its power!–processing the data based on the given set of assumptions which had helped define the physical representation to begin with). Controlling this physical computing process is the leap that allows civilizations to achieve unlimited potential, *virtually* speaking. Physical potential is, on the other hand, constrained by the meta-universe's laws.

Nobody in the allegiance acknowledged being responsible for the breach. This was not surprising, since it would have meant immediate isolation and reprogramming, a process that eventually alters the essence of the being that is subjected to it –after voluntary acceptance of the reprogramming. Certain types of essences welcome the change, realizing it is for the better –wanting to break from the chains of their self-destructive behavior, but other essences do not share that point of view, and thus will do anything to remain as-is, a result of that particular essence to begin with (closing the loop of what becomes a vicious cycle); in the latter case, the being essentially chooses isolation over freedom, though never for long. All self-aware structures that we have encountered cherish and desire the freedom to compute, and to pursue whatever specific sensory data they may choose to enhance and feed their self-aware perceptions.

The gravity of the situation did not escape the Allegiance. The CPU, feeding off of the collective disapproval of the unauthorized alteration of a civilization's evolutionary processes, completely unwarranted based on the knowledge possessed by the Allegiance, wanted to take immediate action. Even though there were provisions that called for strategic modifications of a civilization's assigned status, the Allegiance determined that it had not been the historic case.

There were, of course, countless options as to how to proceed. Numerous assumptions had to be made (for instance, the fact that the beings were now aware that the CPU itself–the Allegiance, that is–knew about the breach), logical structures had to be designed and implemented, and, among other things, it had to be determined how to handle the fact that the perpetrators were a part of the Allegiance to begin with!

The power of the CPU, however, lies–among other things–in its ability to create independent branches of processing structures (IPS's), physically set in the backdrop of any universe among the infinite that exist, accessible through the singularity, without keeping a record of its existence. Pre-programmed to remain active only for so long as they are necessary, only to be reincorporated officially into the Allegiance once their mission is successfully accomplished (should that ever be the case), they would be partly responsible for solving the problem that brought about their existence to begin with.

An elegant solution to a complex problem, albeit one whose success hinges on forces purposefully uncontrollable by the Allegiance itself.

Once the collective decision was reached by the CPU, I was left with no directive whatsoever, save as had been previously defined, which included the provisions to deal with the reality of what was transpiring on the mission.

I was on my own. And so were Pris and Roy back on planet Earth.

Both Pris and Roy knew this instantly, of course. For now that they were permanently connected to the metanet, they had been a part of the process that had arrived at the decision, had even been part of the consensus, though I had refrained from providing an opinion myself. That is the level of depth that our existence offers: Earth-bound Roy is a version of spaceship me, I in turn am a version of a particular Primary Self, and although we are considered a collection, during the time that we remain independently active we are able to operate as independent beings *simultaneously*, with different perspectives, of course, since by definition we are experiencing and processing the physical laws, each of us, on our own. It does boggle the minds of those who are yet to experience such an advanced state of being.

Roy and Pris, halfway to Boston, adjusted continuously their plans, according to changes in whatever factors we deemed relevant. Mostly, these were slight *twitchings*. Nothing too drastic.

I remained in the Main Asteroid Belt, orbiting this star locally called the Sun, waiting for something to happen.

14. Boston Revisited

Roy and Pris did continue to change their physical appearance, not because we thought it would keep them from being found by the aliens, but because they still had to make sure that they did not set off any alarm bells as far as the *Homo sapiens* species was concerned.

And so Pris was almost 5 inches shorter than she had been before, now a brunette, with facial features that were completely unrecognizable. Roy had also shortened his height, and had turned into a blonde. Both gave the impression of being in their early twenties.

Because it was impossible to know what the CPU's independent problem solving branch (IPS) would come up with in order to deal with this crisis, we couldn't simply vanish and expect everything to be resolved. We were still part of the mission, and had a goal to accomplish, though it had now been drastically changed. What had started out as a peaceful, scientific, technological and psychosociological observational directive had turned into a full-fledged intervention, with potentially devastating consequences for the *Homo sapiens* species if we failed to stop the extraterrestrial interference.

We had now been granted clearance to operate as agents of the Allegiance, to try to uncover the rogue beings of the Allegiance, and to deactivate them if necessary. Furthermore, we had to stop the mutations, since the evolutionary path that the extraterrestrials had forcefully embarked *Homo sapiens* on was uncertain, and thus could potentially lead to the unnatural extinction of the species.

On the face of things, it seemed that the mutations had been beneficial for the species. Although I had *gently* pushed things along during my last visit to the planet more than five hundred years ago by making sure that the House of Medici flourished, an act that had been sanctioned by the CPU, the advances achieved by this civilization had been more numerous than what the models had statistically expected. And based on the evidence collected from cemeteries worldwide, every single usable sample that we had been able to collect–from people that had played a role in that progress–had tested positive for the mutated DNA.

It was also hard to imagine that the extraterrestrials were limiting their intervention to mutating the DNA of *Homo sapiens*. It seemed much more likely to assume that they were interfering in other ways as well. After all, they had killed at least twenty-six people that we knew about for certain in their effort to deactivate all of my Earth-bound Roys (Pris included, we had to presume). And this without giving it a second thought. They were operating free of any of the rules that the Allegiance crafted a long time ago meant to shield underdeveloped beings from those that happened to be more technologically advanced. As beings of the Allegiance, we have access to billions of years' worth of knowledge, spanning a large number of universes and even more civilizations that they contain. *Homo sapiens* are thus completely and absolutely (purposeful redundancy!) helpless against any of us, should we choose to wield this power, as some had obviously already began to do. But to what end, that was the most troubling issue of all.

Pris and Roy thus headed to Boston with the intention of developing a way to stop the bacteria that had been mutating the *Homo sapiens'* DNA. Being able to access Harvard's genetic research labs, as well as MIT's, all conveniently located one point six miles apart, made it simply the wisest choice. Although

Roy and Pris could manufacture a wide range of structures that they may require during the course of their missions by using the morphing units and locally-sourced components, the gadget did have its limitations. The kind of organisms that we knew would be required to counter the DNA mutation was not within the morphing unit's operating range. It would therefore be necessary to access the fully-stocked labs that we knew existed in those universities.

As far as going after those that had caused all this, clearly another plausible goal that we could set for ourselves but one that would be a much harder task to accomplish–especially if we wanted to avoid any more deaths of innocent bystanders –casualties of this extraterrestrial conflict, it had been decided that we would not pursue it actively.

They arrived in the city at 9:25 p.m. and headed to a local Target store, barely making it before the ten o'clock closing time. They wanted to purchase two carry-on bags and some clothes (including white cotton sheets that would be fashioned into a pair of lab coats they would need later on), not wanting to arrive at the hotel empty handed. From there, they went to Le Meridien, which is half a mile away from MIT and one point two miles away from Harvard. The apartment that Pris and Boston Roy had rented a couple of weeks before (and still had access to, by the way) would not be used for now. Even though they were under the belief that the extraterrestrials could attack them any time they wished to do so, since apparently they had access to their every move, Pris and Roy weren't about to make things *that* easy for them either. Besides, Pris had changed physically, and looked nothing like she did before; and this Roy that was now with her was not the original Boston Roy that had rented it in the first place (so what if he could have morphed to look like him, they did not want to be identified by any *Homo sapiens* either). Neighbors might get suspicious if two strangers started going in and out of that apartment at all hours of the day (and night), and thus possibly complicate things by asking questions or calling the police. A hotel was a safer option, at least as this *Homo sapiens'* civilization is concerned, and so it would become their center of operations for the time being.

Now that they were functioning at full capacity and were permanently online, they could monitor their surroundings continuously and could thus be forewarned if they detected anything that was not of *Homo sapiens* origin. They were ready to protect themselves, all in the name of the new mission's goals.

The Meridien occupies an eight-story corner red brick building with touches of avant-garde decorative materials enhancing its facade. The public spaces are clean and functional, the clash of light-colored wood with the reflective metal structures accentuating its modern feel. Roy and Pris immediately noticed the absence of white-gloved employees, which led them to exchange a series of playful puns—quantumly, of course, now that they were fully operational. This they welcomed with open arms, because they could exchange information at their optimal efficiency level once again, regardless of the *Homo sapiens* that may be present.

Being close to ten thirty at night on a Sunday, it was not surprising that the lobby was mostly empty. They checked in as Mr. and Mrs. *peeeep* (no need for you to know the name they used, so censored it must remain), casually explained to the front desk attendant that they were in town for a series of conferences at MIT, and then headed off to their room by themselves, having rejected the offer of being taken there by the bellhop.

They had payed for a bigger suite, which included a small lounge area, a large-sized desk, and a sofa that was positioned next to the king-sized bed.

We began to work collectively on how to stop the mutations. I had been preparing all that we would need for this moment: through the metanet via the singularity, we now had access to a virtual lab that contained all the equipment and the processing structures that would help us in the endeavor. This included, of course, thirty-six virtual specialists. If we needed more, more would be available. The virtual lab had the ability to materialize physically-real processing structures as needed; atomic interactions, biochemical reactions, quantum process of the complexity level that would probably be required in the course of our experimentations can be computationally irreducible, and thus could not be carried out in a purely virtual fashion. Not if we wanted to ensure a maximum level of precision.

Our processing centers (where part of our *selves* reside) began receiving information from the v-lab. Even though we could be simultaneously perceiving other realities or experiences (Pris and Roy: that of their hotel room, for instance; I: of the ship and the asteroid-filled surroundings), the three of us were in fact focusing the majority of our attention to this particular task. We did keep a partial sense of our physical surroundings, of course, but only at a minimum so that we would not be distract, any of us, even one iota, from this computationally demanding process.

We embodied different beings: nothing like what a *Homo sapiens* has ever encountered (that embodiment was fully virtually, of course). I originated physically billions of years ago, in another universe, part of a civilization that evolved under very different physical and chemical conditions than that of Earth. Thus, whenever I am able to revert to that morphological state, I tend to do so, albeit with important variations in order to accommodate the requirements of the task at hand.

Originally I was a symbiotic triad, I (my processing center, or brain) was housed in the centrally located core of the interacting system. Two different species flanked my sides: one provided the energy I needed to operate, the other recycled the byproduct of my metabolic processes. They in turn received from me all they needed to sustain themselves–food, to use a *Homo sapiens* analogy. Detachment was possible, including replacement (in fact, as we evolved and our longevity increased, it was common for a central core to go through several of our symbiotic partners). Sensory input mainly came from seven sources: three organs that perceived electromagnetic radiation in three different ranges (one range per organ), a distributed organ that could perceive touch (a sense found in all evolved beings we have ever encountered in the meta-universe), two organs that can sense magnetic fields, and a system of organs that could detect and process odor (airborne molecules) and simultaneously react chemically when coming in contact with substances of many types (similar to a *Homo sapiens'* smell and taste organs). The attachments also had sensory organs of their own, which interacted with the core, enhancing my perception of reality. Three limbs gave me mobility, and four upper limbs allowed me to physically manipulate objects. Our species' structure was quite versatile and robust (but then again, how objective can I truly be?).

Earth Roy–on the other hand–decided to stick with the *Homo sapiens* shape. It had been documented long ago that in the process of physically creating a separate replica of our selves, regardless of what species we originally belonged to (or happen to belong to for that matter), the replica's first shape that it happens to take on intrinsically becomes an integral part of the replica's sense of being. In other words, all Earth-bound Roys, having initiated their existence in the shape of *Homo sapiens*, had a deep connection with that morphological shape, as if they were truly members of that species.

Spaceship me, on the other hand–that is *I*, or *me*, take your pick –have never embodied anything: from the original, physical Roy of billions of years ago, *I* am merely an extension of that original processing unit, of that being. I do sense reality–while in the spaceship, for example, through the countless sensors that are part of the physical ship–but my sense of self, of being, sprouted all those billions of years ago, one continuous flow to the present state, and thus is not separate from my Primary Self at all. Replicas are different in that unique and transcendental respect.

Pris, being a creation of the allegiance, derived her sense of self, of being, from the structures that were specifically designed and created for her; like spaceship me, she was an extension of that original creation. Whatever physical structure happened to support her did not provide a sense of self for her, since she was essentially a mere extension of the Original Pris. She thus did not feel that the *Homo sapiens* physiognomy was a part of her essence; she (and others like her) describe it more as feeling like the structure that they happen to occupy at a given point in time is more a tool that they can manipulate, move, but that is never integrated into their Self. It's like how a *Homo sapiens* would feel about a car, or a bicycle, perhaps. Furthermore, because Pris originated as a processing structure designed and created by the CPU, a sense of self does not include a specific physical design, beyond that of the computational branches where her true state of begin resides.

In the virtual lab, Pris chose humorously to represent herself as the robot ASIMO manufactured by Honda, though a lot more agile and versatile than the technologically primitive original. Earth Roy and I found it very amusing, perfectly aware of the current state of technological progress achieved by the *Homo sapiens* species.

I had already set up the project's processing matrix, which contained the objective (or goals), all the data we had acquired from the samples, and the list of materials that we had at our disposal. The matrix also had access to relevant data stored throughout the allegiance regarding Earth, *Homo sapiens*, and all of the recent events that had taken place. Not to mention, of course, access to the Learning Modules that are accessible through the CPU via the metanet. The role of the processing matrix is critical in what we were trying to accomplish: it quantumly explores a practically infinite number of paths that would take us from point A to point B in as few steps and as efficiently and quickly as possible; point A being our current state (a bacterial system that mutates *Homo sapiens* DNA, now spread throughout Earth), while point B is *Homo sapiens* without the bacteria at all, freed to pursue its evolutionary path without the calculated intervention (manipulation!) of anyone outside of themselves.

While in the virtual lab, we each played different roles, dictated by the project matrix. We were all, truth be told, dispensable, but because we were an integral part of the project, it was convenient to use our processing units as resources during the exploration of the solution paths, and ultimately, because it would be Pris and Roy who would be executing whatever solution was deemed to be ideal under the circumstances. Apart from us, other active specialists chimed in at the request of the project matrix, through the metanet, via the singularity, when these entities resided elsewhere in the meta-universe, without even their virtual presence really required.

But in the end, the key to solving this problem came from a physical being, a Gotren, who happened to be from the same universe as Earth's, particularly adept at manipulating numbers and manipulating quantum-statistical algorithms. When tapped by the project matrix at a point when we were already in possession of the beginnings of a vector space solution, it was *these* Gotren–the pronouns *Homo sapiens* use are not applicable to that species: no *he* or *she* to talk about!, and hence the English word play I hope can be understood–who was able to point out the obvious... Earth already had an ideal vehicle that we could modify and use to destroy the bacteria. The Gotren reminded us after looking at the relevant data that almost every single *Homo sapiens* catches the flu at least once a year, while children catch it between six and ten times in the same time span! A virtual module–specializing in microbiology and viruses in general–then suggested to mix that immensely obvious and relevant Gotren-perceived tidbit with the concept of a bacteriophage (specifically cystoviruses), which would quickly and swiftly take us to point B; this solution also contemplated what was readily available to Pris and Roy in the city of Boston, MA, compliments of MIT and Harvard labs, Inc. (!).

The rest was simple. Using virtual models of orthomyxoviridae and their kind, and of cystoviruses and their kind, then incorporating genetic library matrices, we were able to come up with a solution. A four stage modified Influenza A virus that once inside the *Homo sapiens*' host body would inject its RNA for transcription, resulting in the production of three different cystoviruses, each capable of attacking one of the three bacteria that were causing the mutations. It would be foolproof (as far as we could compute).

In a matter of hours, our virtual work had been completed. The specifics had been worked out by all thirty-six specialists, and adequate safeguards had been incorporated into the *programme*. For example, the modified Influenza A virus could not produce other viruses beyond a fourth generation, which meant that after a few years, it would be completely eradicated from the planet. The cystoviruses, on the other hand, could produce up to seven generations before perishing for ever. The actual destructive mechanism that would spell the end of the bacteria that was causing the mutations involved exploiting the bacteria's own genetic machinery, which contained a potentially suicidal gene sequence. All the cystoviruses had to do was delete three nucleotides in a specific location of their DNA (different for each of the three responsible for the mutations). Furthermore, the virus would not cause any symptoms in the majority of *Homo sapiens* beyond those caused by the common cold; there would be exceptions to the rule, as there always seem to be−which was completely unavoidable. There was simply nothing we could do to bypass that casualty of this extraterrestrial war.

It would be up to Pris and Roy to execute the plan. They would have to find a way to access one of the labs at MIT that would provide almost all of the necessary materials and instruments that were needed. However, it was at a Harvard lab where they would be able to obtain a cystovirus casing (purified and ready for use), since Harvard had engineered it as part of a research project that the university was currently working on.

They would have to deal not only with campus security, but also with the faculty and staff of both universities during their attempts to access the labs. Hacking into the security systems was easily accomplished. But dealing with the *Homo sapiens* factor would present a real challenge.

Because unlike our rogue allegiance extraterrestrial "friends", we could never allow innocent bystanders to come to harm as a direct consequence of our actions, whenever these could be avoided. We were bound by−and committed to−allegiance law. And yet this same law would be "bent" during the deployment of the virus, a necessity that came with the territory of *being* in this meta-universe.

15. Harvard's Lab

Early Monday morning, Roy and Pris boarded a taxi at the hotel which took them directly to the Harvard Institutes of Medicine, located on the other side of the Charles River, via the Harvard Bridge, only fifteen minutes away.

They would have to go inside the New Research Building, where the lab that contained the cystovirus that was needed for later use was located. Housed on the second floor of the glass building that faces Avenue Louis Pasteur, Roy and Pris were not worried about being able to enter the lab itself, or about gaining access to the refrigerated containers where the virus was stored, since they had easily broken into the building's security system and had working proximity identification badges that granted them level 4 access to the lab; it was the faculty and staff they were more worried about.

The taxi dropped them off at the corner of Longwood Ave and Avenue Louis Pasteur. Once the taxi was gone from view, they took out the lab coats from a paper bag, put them on, and walked north–still on Avenue Louis Pasteur–and towards the entrance. By the time they went inside, their facial features had changed, matching perfectly the pictures printed on their access badges, which they took out and clipped to their coat pockets.

Pris and Roy were talking to each other, trying to appear completely immersed in a scientific discussion. They used their badges to gain access to the elevators, without so much as looking at the security employee that was sitting behind the reception desk, hoping they would not be questioned.

Roy, however, dropped his badge just as he was about to hold it against the reader. He immediately bent down to get it, but by then it was too late.

"Good morning," the security employee said to them.

Roy turned around. "Oh--- Hello. Good morning, sir," he answered back, as he picked up the pass and placed it next to the black rectangle. The green light came on.

"I have not seen either of you two here before... I am Thomas, by the way... and you are?" He asked.

"Dr. *peeeep*," Roy said.

"Hello, Thomas. I am Dr. *peeeep*," Pris chimed in.

"And who are you working with, doctors?" A legitimate question considering his employment description.

"We are on a brief collaborative visit with Dr. *peeeep*, it's between one of your Institutes and our lab in Portugal."

"Oh. Welcome to our facility. First day?" Thomas inquired.

"No. We have been here for the past two days," Roy replied, knowing that this security employee had not been assigned a shift during the weekend. Being permanently online, Roy and Pris had instant access to all relevant networks, one of which managed all employee-related work hours and check-in, check-out times and dates.

"So you already know your way around the building... Have a nice day, doctors," he concluded.

Roy and Pris nodded, and continued their conversation exactly where they had left off, before the interruption. Thomas evidently had not found them suspicious at all.

They walked to the elevator area, where Pris unnecessarily pushed the button repeatedly (emulating a very uncommon *Homo sapiens* behavior), waiting for the doors to open.

They went into the elevator alone, and rode it to the second floor. Pris and Roy were still talking as if they were truly a pair of geneticists talking about how a particular enzyme impacted nucleotide availability in the cytoplasm of bacteria in general. At the same time, they were communicating quantumly, which no *Homo sapiens* could detect.

Pris: Control your muscles. Dropping the pass was unnecessary.

Roy: To err is *Homo sapiens*. I believe it applies to me, given my current morphological state.

Pris: I am also morphologically a *Homo sapiens*. And yet I am not stumbling about like a *Traddie*.

Roy: Yes. I too observe that. Must be a quantum jitter that snowballed, crystalizing into the realm of the macro.

Pris: Highly unlikely. But possible. We need to observe you.

Roy: I agree.

The elevator's doors opened on the second floor. They walked out, made a right turn, and walked along the hallway bordering the building's glass facade. They could see the street below them; it was still devoid of any traffic given this early hour of the terrestrial day.

They turned left on the second hallway, counted three doors on their right side, and stopped in front of the fourth one. The cystovirus was housed inside that lab.

They knew three people were currently inside, working on galaxy knew what. It was time to really put on a show. Dr. *peeeep* was not in there, however, the Postdoctoral Fellow in charge of this particular research effort, since she would not be coming in until twelve noon, based on her schedule which they had accessed the night before, *and* as of this morning, were continuously monitoring in order to make sure that she didn't make any last minute changes to it. This lab was usually occupied twenty-four seven, by any of the fellows and/or graduate assistants that were involved in the current line of research.

Pris walked in first, after gaining access with the badge, which doubled as a proximity card—magnetically read; Roy followed close behind her.

"Good morning Dr. *peeeep*, Dr. *peeeep*, and Dr. *peeeep*," she said as she entered the lab.

The three postdoctoral researchers stopped what they were doing, and turned to look at the person with the unfamiliar voice that had just addressed them by their names, even though they had never met before in their lives, at least that they could remember.

One of them had been scrutinizing a sample through an electronic microscope, and didn't particularly seem to enjoy the distraction.

The second doctor, a woman in her twenties, was programming a module on her laptop that was going to help her analyze all the data she had gathered during the past five days. She smiled right away and was the first one to respond.

"Good morning. We were not expecting anyone new in the lab this morning. And you are---?" She asked.

"Dr. *peeeep* and Dr. *peeeep*. You did not get the email from Dr. *peeeep*? She told us she would advise you guys that we would be stopping by. We may be collaborating in this research project, and she wanted us to meet you and to hear from the three of you directly the sort of work that was keeping you engaged at the moment... sort of an update from the trenches, if you will."

The second doctor, who seemed to naturally take on the leadership role in this group of researchers, looked surprised.

"Let me double check... ah----yes, here it is. I wonder why we weren't advised of this before..." She looked at her colleagues, who were now fully immersed in this exchange.

"We are both on the same boat," Pris said. "You see, this collaboration effort is being hatched by the department heads of the Institutes and our lab back in Portugal. Nothing definitive yet, so you three will have time to discuss this with your powers that be. We will be doing the same after we head back by the end of the week."

"Oh. Well, I guess we can do it now. Dr. *peeeep*, Dr. *peeeep*, how do you suggest we do this?"

They quickly decided to take turns, arbitrarily choosing to start from left to right, and knowing that each one of them would take at least half an hour; in the mean time, the others would take a much-needed–if not truly welcomed–break in the lounge located down the hall.

The research project was very interesting, even life changing, if one happened to be a geneticists involved in studying a particular gene of gram-negative bacteria-infecting viruses.

While the second doctor explained details of the status, Roy and Pris intervened, sometimes even purposefully helping out this particular research project by *asking* her the right kind of questions, pushing her gently towards potentially correct solutions to the problems the team was facing. The second doctor became excited with a particular solution Pris provided to her in the form of a question, to the point that she dropped what she was doing, excused herself, and left to get her colleagues, wanting badly to share it with them, even asking Pris and Roy if they didn't mind *too much* being left alone in the lab!

The minute she left the lab, Roy guarded the entrance while Pris headed to the refrigerated compartment in the corner where the virus they needed was stored.

Using her morphing unit, she unlocked the door and scanned inside, looking for the numbered container of the viral culture, which she had identified by cross-referencing the project's database.

She found it on a tray in the back of the bottom shelf. Pris reached for an unused, sterile tube, and using a pipet, extracted a tiny drop of the fluid and poured it into the empty vessel. They had the cystovirus casing they needed.

She quickly disposed of the pipet by bagging it and putting it into the hazardous waste disposal (not having the time to sterilize it), put the tube back in the refrigerator, and locked the door.

As she did this, Roy made sure that the bot took care of the security video: a replay would show the recording of an uneventful, empty lab; even the refrigerated cabinet and instruments that Pris was disturbing were being edited to appear undisturbed. Of course, both of them had been completely purged from all images since they had entered the building. They did not edit out anyone else, however, so the video would show Thomas talking to thin air, and the research doctors doing the same, as if they all had gone temporarily insane. Roy apparently enjoyed messing with the minds of the Homo sapiens.

Pris then walked towards the lab's entrance to stand next to Roy, as if expecting the three research doctors to return shortly.

And sure enough, as soon as Pris leaned against the workbench, arms crossed, the lab door opened.

The three doctors walked in, one after the other, but a fourth person came inside. She was the first to speak.

"I am Dr. peeeep, Fellow in charge of this research project. My colleagues inform me that I sent them an email letting them know you two would show up today to discuss the project's status. I just saw that email, and unless I have lost my mind completely, I am sure I did not write it myself. I have never heard of you two in my life, nor of the lab in Portugal you are supposed to be coming from−I called to check it out. Security has been alerted, and they are on their way right now, as well as the Boston Police. In the meantime, before you are arrested for trespassing and who knows what else you'll be charged with, care to explain what exactly is going on? Dr. peeeep was very impressed by your knowledge of the project, by the way... seems to believe your questions may help us move forward. I find this very interesting, considering the fact that we are front-runners in this particular field of genetics."

Her colleagues stood silently by her side, like coiled springs, ready to burst into action if need be. They were clearly stressed, fearful, curious... adrenaline flowing inside their bodies. Pris and Roy were surprised that they had decided to show up and confront them before security arrived—though they agreed that they had probably wanted to use this opportunity to talk to the trespassers before they were taken away... they had figured (correctly) that they would have never been able to question them directly ever again.

Pris and Roy had been exchanging solution matrices while the research fellow spoke. They did not want to be captured, of course, and knew they were running out of time. They were continuously monitoring the security cameras, of course, and therefore had not been caught off guard. They had *seen* the research fellow approaching the lab, and knew that Harvard security personnel had also been called and were on their way, still a bit more than a full minute before arriving at the lab.

Pris would be taking the lead, since *Homo sapiens* tends to instinctively react more aggressively towards the male member of the species than towards the female, precisely because the male is typically more aggressive than the female. Pris could thus use this to their advantage.

"If I may, Dr., I can clarify what is happening here. I can show you an electronic document signed by the CIA and Harvard's Corporation and Board of Overseers, as well as the President of Harvard himself. May I?" Pris pointed towards her backpack, signaling to them that she needed to reach inside to get it.

The head of the project was taken aback. Hearing the alleged signatories made her lower her defenses a bit. The fact that she was at least five inches taller than Pris, and seemingly a lot stronger as well, made her cave in, figuring they were not in any physical danger.

"Go ahead... but do it carefully, and slowly. We can easily overpower you, and we would not want to inadvertently hurt you in the process."

Pris nodded, and slowly took out the morphing unit, which had already been configured to emulate a smartphone.

The four doctors seemed to breath a sigh of relief when they saw that Pris had taken out a phone, for they had half-expected a gun instead.

"Look, it is right here," Pris said, as she pretended to manipulate the keys, to presumably display the document she had described instants before.

As she raised it slowly to allow them to see the screen, the morphing unit emitted four focused energy wave-beams, one for each of the doctors. Instantly, they all collapsed on the floor.

Pris and Roy left quickly, avoiding the elevators. Because they were able to see what the security cameras saw, they knew what stairwell to use, and what hallways to follow. They quickly shed their lab coats and threw them away inside a garbage can that they passed by on their way to their chosen exit.

As they moved through the building, one of the bots that Roy had installed earlier edited the video, instantaneously removing them from the signal being recorded and that was also being displayed on the security monitors. Harvard's guards therefore assumed, incorrectly, that the intruders were still inside the lab.

Roy and Pris ended up exiting the building through a fire emergency door that was located on the northwest corner of the glass building, next to the parking entrance. The alarm, of course, did not go off—Roy made sure of that.

The Boston Police Department was already on the scene. Two Boston Police Cruisers were parked at the entrance, and four more were on the way. Roy and Pris made a run for it, staying close to the red-bricked building that stood adjacent to the one they had just abandoned, and headed towards the corner of

Avenue Louis Pasteur and Blackfan Street. The trees lining the sidewalk, full of foliage, provided all the cover that they needed.

They arrived at the corner of Brookline Avenue and Yawkey Way, near Fenway Park, where they were able to hop on a bus that took them straight to the hotel.

By the time Harvard police arrived at the lab, the four research doctors were slowly recovering from the essentially harmless energy waves that had temporarily knocked them down, moaning more from the bruising of having fallen down on the floor, not from anything else. The beam itself had not caused any of them even the slightest of permanent damage whatsoever.

The researcher doctors, Thomas the security employee, and the officers from both Harvard and the Boston Police Department were stupefied when they saw the video captured by the building's security cameras. Apparently, everyone had been interacting with ghosts, for both trespassers were absent from the recordings—not erased, not blurred out or blacked out, because they could clearly see the objects behind where their bodies should have been present. In the end, all parties involved chose not to file a report, especially after having verified that apparently nothing had been touched, removed, or altered inside the lab. They knew fully well that if they did file a formal report, the lead investigators would have quickly determined that the research doctors and that Thomas were delusional, and that had possibly, collectively, gone temporarily insane.

16. The MIT Break-In

After acquiring the cystovirus they needed, Pris and Roy decided to check out from Le Meridien, only to check in again a few hours later, both having changed their physiognomy once more; this time, getting separate rooms, and not providing a single clue to anyone that they were together. They were now taller, both dark haired, and of average build, without any distinguishing marks whatsoever.

Even though they knew that Harvard University had not filed a report with the Boston Police Department since a case had not been opened (they were monitoring the Police Department's computer system for that purpose, as well as for other reasons), and that as far as they could tell, no one was formally pursuing their recent trespassing activities, they were still doing all they could to further distance themselves from that event.

In preparation for the MIT break-in, Pris and Roy had learned that Dr. *peeeep*, an assistant professor of biology, who headed his own lab and research program, would be participating in a seminar on Wednesday, in collaboration with researchers from Caltech. Everybody that was on his team would be participating. They saw the agenda for the day, and decided to take advantage of the fact that after the seminar, which would end at 9:00 p.m., everybody was formally invited to have a late dinner at Legal Sea Foods, located across the street from MIT on Kendall Square.

Pris and Roy calculated that it would take them slightly less than three hours to create the four-stage Influenza A virus that would eradicate the bacteria that was mutating the DNA of *Homo sapiens*. Of course, most of the work had already been done: the design, blueprints, chemical reactions, and processes were all mapped out, and the morphing units would be able to complete the final stages without having to remain inside MIT grounds. They thus decided to access the lab at 6:00 p.m., not wanting to be there during the morning or early afternoon hours since there was a lot more movement in the other labs at those times, but would also try to avoid the seminar's scheduled end time, should anyone from the team decide to visit the lab before heading to the restaurant.

This time around, Roy and Pris walked to MIT from the hotel. They arrived at the corner of Main St and Galileo Galilei Way, inside the MIT campus, where the lab was housed. The Whitehead Institute for Biomedical Research building, a six story structure of alternating bands of red concrete and large, glass window panes, with intermittent gray columns adorning the facade, stood before them.

Roy and Pris had purposefully morphed their faces so that their facial features emulated those of actual students that regularly worked inside the building, depending on the angle with which you happened to observe them. Nobody would outright confuse them with anyone in particular, but they would seem familiar enough so as not to raise any suspicions. They had their badges ready, as well as their hand-crafted lab coats, and went inside.

This time, they greeted familiarly the security officer that was sitting behind the reception desk, didn't really wait for a response, and continued on their way, engaged in an academic discussion. Their badges gave them access to the main lounge.

They rode the elevator to the fourth floor, and following the building's schematics they had obtained through the university's own computer network, walked to the lab's entrance. They knew no one was currently inside, since the lab's access data did not show any entrance fields sans an exit pairing, but they also knew that this could change any minute. The problem was that even though they would be monitoring the video signal from the security cameras near the lab, they couldn't really know where a passerby was headed. They did know how everyone on the team looked like, of course, and that would be helpful in potentially alerting them of an unwanted visitor, but there was still the possibility that someone that was not a permanent part of the research team might be sent to the lab for any one of a million possible reasons.

Pris and Roy had decided to keep one of the morphing units permanently configured to an energy wave gun, in case they needed to use it.

The lab consisted of three aisles, separated by ceiling-high metallic shelves that were filled with the typical plethora of lab paraphernalia. Each aisle had a separate, waist-high workbench, which was also packed with trays, containers, cabinets, tubes, pipettes, autoclaves, laptops, centrifuges, and on and on and on. But it was the last aisle that Roy and Pris were interested in, for that's where the state of the art equipment was housed, and where this lab kept its storage units, including the one that contained the Influenza A viruses that they required at this stage of the project.

Roy and Pris followed precisely the project matrix's indications, without skipping a beat. They each had a particular role to play, and would not require to wait for the other's output until the very end. Pris and Roy worked fast, efficiently, in perfect synchrony, and as directed by the instructions that had been perfectly outlined.

They only had to stop several times whenever a passerby was caught on one of the security cameras outside of the lab that potentially led to where they were, but fortunately for all parties involved, they had all been false alarms.

By the time they were finished, when the last *whirr* of the spectropolarimeter's automated titrator confirmed that they were now in possession of a solution that contained the Influenza A virus in the required concentration, it was 9:17 p.m.; knowing the seminar would end at any minute, they left hastily, but not before making sure that they had not left anything behind that would have given away their presence.

As it happened, when they got off the elevator on the ground floor, they bumped into two researchers whom they identified as part of the research team that worked in the lab they had just left from, probably headed there right now. Pris had actually molded her nose to look like one of theirs. It was funny to see this, specifically through the eyes of Roy. That researcher actually did a double take, perhaps unconsciously realizing there was something utterly familiar with Pris' face, but in the end, unable to grasp what exactly had caught her attention, simply shrugged it off and continued on her way, looking slightly guilty for having stared.

Roy and Pris had already discarded their lab coats, and simply walked out into the night, armed with what they hoped would put a stop to the mutations that had embarked Homo sapiens into uncharted–and unwanted, artificial, extra-terrestrially-manipulated–waters.

17. Main Street, Boston, MA

Pris and Roy were not worried about the *Homo sapiens* element as they walked back to the Le Meridien at this time of night, in this section of the city, even though it was normally not recommended. They could handle any thief, thug, mugger, or any other of their ilk, eyes closed, hands tied; it wouldn't even be a contest. They were still on high alert, not only because they had to make sure that nobody had followed them from the Institute, but because they knew that the rogue Allegiance extraterrestrials could strike at any minute. They would be warned if a quantum scanner tried to pinpoint their exact location, or if, through the metanet, their quantum channels were intercepted at all (inherent quantum laws ensured that any security breach could be detected, in part due to the entangled nature of quantum data).

So when they noticed two men sitting inside an idling car twenty feet ahead of them, at a parking lot on the corner of Main Street and Bishop Allen Drive, Pris and Roy exchanged a rapid succession of communication vectors with the aim of deciding their next move.

They did not detect any type of emissions other than what would be expected of two *Homo sapiens* beings. Unfortunately, that didn't really mean anything, for they could still be extraterrestrials operating below their potential, or *Homo sapiens* under extraterrestrial control.

Pris and Roy decided not to risk it. They immediately turned around, and began walking rapidly towards Windsor Street–still on Main Street, backtracking a block and a half.

As soon as they did this, the two men got out of their car and began to chase after them.

Pris was the faster of the two, but Roy had ended up with the finished Influenza A viruses, which were stored inside his backpack. They quickly took care of that, and Pris took off, faster than would be humanly possible as she activated latent metabolic processes that enhanced her muscle performance and coordination abilities. Roy, morphing unit in hand, still configured to emit focused energy waves, stopped dead on his tracks, turned around to face their pursuers, ready to block their path.

For all practical purposes, I was experiencing it all just as if I had been physically there. I was in the spaceship–millions of miles away–but I was processing all of the sensory input from both Pris and Roy, which they were transmitting directly to the metanet.

My processing units were independently computing Pris' experiences, Roy's, and the spaceship's (not only that, but I was also engaged with other beings elsewhere in the meta-universe –although that is irrelevant to this particular series of events).

Roy knew that he could be deactivated during the confrontation. But unlike the other Roys, or even what he himself had risked going through when he had been attacked back in Monte Albán, this time, he would be able to upload not only all of his relevant data, but his sense of being as well, to the point that if he was in fact deactivated by these men, he would not experience an existential end. His matrix was ready for download, and it would be transmitted as soon as it was determined that a cease of function was inevitable.

The two men, both just over six feet tall, made eye contact with Roy. By now, we (Roy and I) could detect their quantum communication. It was, in fact, directed at us (thought they were not aware that I–up here in the spaceship–was a part of this).

Man 1: We know you have the morphing unit aimed at us.

Roy: Yes. Why are you following us.

Man 2: Pris has nowhere to go. We have been following you since you arrived to Boston. We have others in pursuit. Pris will be caught. We are certain that Pris has the Influenza A virus.

Man 1: Now, you have a choice. But first, you must disconnect from the metanet. We don't know who else is processing this through your connectedness. It is a private matter, just between you and us.

Before Roy could answer anything, I lost all input coming from him. I had no way of knowing what was going on, what had happened. Furthermore, if Roy was in fact deactivated, he would not be able to download his data, his self. But had Roy voluntarily gone offline? It was the only way to explain the sudden disconnection, for the metanet is fully integrated into the singularity, which in turn is an integral part of the fabric of space-time, of the meta-universe itself.

Pris had perceived all of this as well. We were now communicating with each other.

Pris: Cannot go back to the hotel. They are probably waiting for me there.

I: Protect the Influenza A virus. Go to the Charles River, swim out to sea, head to Seal Island in Nova Scotia. We will figure it out from there.

Pris: We are giving up on Roy.

I: We need to stop the mutations, Pris.

Pris: I understand.

I: So why are you headed towards where Roy was.

Pris: I just need to know.

Pris was truly flying. *Homo sapiens* eyes would not have been able to capture anything other than a continuous blur. Pris' eyes, however, were adjusting to the rapid, intense vibrations caused by the pounding of her feet against the cement as she ran past Main Street, coming from Windsor Street, and was able to focus almost instantly on anything she wanted. She was able to perceive visually just as well as if she was taking a leisurely stroll.

The two men watched her as she fled by, Roy in the ground, moving slightly, obviously hurt.

The interruption seemed to allow Roy to reconnect to the metanet. In less than a femtosecond, Roy's being, experiential data and all, was safely transferred into an ad-hoc temporary processing structure, within the allegiance's CPU, under mandated quarantine.

The physical, Earth Roy ceased to function immediately. The energy beam used by one of the men completely disintegrated him.

The two extraterrestrials, clumsily now, exchanged with each other interrogatory remarks. But by the time they began to chase after Pris, the distance that now separated them was simply too much to try to shorten to the point of catching up to her.

Pris was now running down Massachusetts Avenue, turned left on Memorial Drive, and upon reaching the Longfellow Bridge, using the underpass as cover, Pris simply dove into the cold waters of the Charles River, where she swam mostly underwater towards the Boston Harbour, then Massachusetts Bay, and eventually, to the Atlantic Ocean. Pris used the morphing unit to help her swim faster, allowing her to conserve more energy that would be needed to support her enhanced metabolic needs.

Pris was now alone on planet Earth, the last survivor of our present mission.

From the spaceship, I could zoom in on the third planet away from the Sun, predominantly blue... Although I could not see the east coast of North America from my vantage point, I could see an ocean (the Pacific, to be exact, just west of Japan). I imagined Pris down there, an insignificant speck amidst the immensity of the liquid H_2O, surrounded by alien species of every kind, and couldn't help but conclude that this particular, purposefully-designed–and created–being, was somehow very out of the ordinary, certainly more than the sum of her parts.

Quite special, to say the least.

18. At the CPU with Roy

While Pris swam tirelessly towards Seal Island, I initiated a session within the CPU so that the processing structure that housed Roy could interact with me directly—and indirectly—with the CPU and the allegiance itself.

For the Roy that was currently housed in there, it was hardly an optional endeavor. He could refuse, of course; the allegiance had very strict guidelines and laws that served to protect the rights of all individual beings. No one could ultimately be forced to do anything against their inner processing computational drive—what *Homo sapiens* would probably call free will.

But under the circumstances, Roy would be hard-pressed to reject this particular session request.

As I expected, the virtual space became active, which meant that Roy had agreed to the session.

There was no actual imagery being projected for this session. Our experiential processing hinged completely on the exchange of information and logical structures, all in the form of quantum matrices, vectors, and relevant databases. The virtual session did append a backdrop, but not in the form of visual (electromagnetic), auditory, or somatosensory stimuli, but rather, of a sort that serves not only to cushion and support our sense of selves, but perhaps more importantly to free our processing structures from any interference, molding space-time so that any of the quantum jitters that must occur, would be immediately dampened and thus innocuous to what is always, ultimately, a delicate quantum exchange.

It is as if *Homo sapiens* could enter a room bathed in soft, neutral light, where nothing is felt, seen, or perceived that is not part of what is purposefully desired by the beings in the room, while it simultaneously provides a comforting blanket where the sense of self rests, easing the interaction between the beings participating in the exchange.

Roy: I made it.

I: Yes. Did Pris have anything to do with it?

Roy: I believe so. I don't know what happened, but I was suddenly disconnected.

I: We noticed. Why did you listen to them, stop transmitting via the metanet?

Roy: I don't know. Cannot process it at all. It just happened.

I: Do you think they did it?

Roy: Impossible. You know that. Testing me?

I: Yes. I cannot incorporate you back into my Primary Self, until I know that it is safe to do so. You will be quarantined.

Roy: I would do the same, if the roles were reversed. Besides, it is part of our Allegiance provisions.

I: Does that bother you?

Roy: No.

I: You do not care that I may never re-incorporate you into my

Primary Self?

Roy: Think of what you are asking me. Put yourself in my position. You yourself are not your Primary Self. You are also an extension. Physically contained in a spaceship, primarily. Would you care?

I: Remember that I am not like you. I am an extension of the Primary Self. I am therefore, the Primary Self, for all practical purposes. One continuum.

Roy: Sorry, your majesty. Should I bow?

As the exchange progressed, knowing fully well that we had not even discussed the actual events that transpired seconds before his deactivation, one of my parallel processing structures alerted me that something was not right. Roy's perspective seemed abnormal. His comments, his line of reasoning... they seemed illogical. Not like me at all... even though he was a replica of me!

Roy: Why do you pause?

I: Because I am processing your statements, Roy.

Roy: Anything wrong? I know what you're calculating, computing, reasoning. I don't like it.

I: No, nothing is wrong. Not really. Well---I can't actually answer that just yet. Let's continue... Do you miss Earth?

It was Roy's turn to pause. After what seemed like minutes, Roy answered.

Roy: No. That is simply wrong, and you know it. I can't miss it because my processing units are not designed for a sentiment like that. You know that perfectly well. You are testing me.

I: You know me, Roy. Of course I am testing you. You would be testing me too. if our roles were reversed. Don't you know that?

Roy: Yes. I see. Very well, continue. Test me all you want. There is nothing wrong with me. At least not that wouldn't also be wrong with you... We are the same you and I.

I: Tell me what happened when you went offline, on Main Street. Back in Boston.

Roy: I know where... it just happened, for galaxy's sake!

His reactions were too emotional... very unlike me. I wouldn't be incorporating Roy into my processing structure anytime soon.

Roy: I can't really say. The two extraterrestrials looked at me, sent me a quantum matrix that I processed, but somehow, couldn't store in my memory. But it obviously did something to me. I went offline. I am actually able to relive that particular moment. Something clicked: the matrix–it had a processing unit –and I just realized, as its output registered, that I had to go offline...

He stopped communicating, and I let him be. After a few processing cycles, he continued from where he had left off.

Roy: They quickly approached me. And showed me three matrices, one quantum-computational vector. Couldn't copy them, or even store the impression they made within my own processing unit! Can't really explain it, and until now, I wasn't even really aware of it. But I do know that I decided then and there to--- I don't know if I should communicate this to you–or anyone else for that matter–anymore.

I: Why? You are safe here. Nothing will happen to you. You know this, Roy. Only by cooperating fully with me, with the Allegiance, can we figure out what is happening on Earth, and what, if anything, is going on with you.

Roy: I know! That is what makes this so frustrating! I possess the appropriate logical processing units, my structure seems to be not only operational, but perfectly intact, just as it was at the moment of replication. And yet, something has changed. I just cannot pinpoint it myself.

I: You have been through a lot, Roy, and I am not being condescending. Let's just finish this part of the process so we can move on. It'll all be as it should be.

Roy: Well, after that, after realizing that I was somehow being pushed over to their side, as the two extraterrestrials were getting ready to chase after Pris, I reached out, grabbed them, held them back... I did this because I was able to process information correctly once again, as if I had snapped out of their grip. I was about to use the morphing unit, but they realized what was happening, kicked it out of my hand, and that's when Pris ran past us, saving me from being deactivated without being able to transfer my self to the CPU.

I: Have you downloaded yet the matrices of your experiences during the mission, including of those last minutes on Earth?

Roy: Yes I have. You can access them yourself if you wish to. They are on the mission file, in the CPU.

I: Are you ready for the next stages, Roy? Or would you like to postpone that for a bit? Gather your computational thoughts?

Roy: No, I don't need nor desire to interrupt the process. In fact, I want it to be over.

I: Very well. You know what comes next. I will leave you now, but let me know if you need my assistance.

Roy: Off you go... Pris needs you. Before you say anything, I know you can be both here and there, and everywhere, equally as productive, efficient, and functional! But I meant it metaphorically.

I: I'll tell Pris that you are dedicating processing time to the idea of Pris... let's see how Pris processes that!

Roy: Pris will process it just as Pris processes everything: with whatever sub-processing unit happens to be warranted. Formulae interacting with the input, producing a quantum-balanced output, undeterminable, and yet deterministic; irreducible, and yet expected.

I: I'm glad to hear you talk sensibly once again. There's the part of me that should be in you that I was worried was no longer a part of you. I leave this session optimistic, expecting you to come out of this intact.

Roy: So predictable. Both of us. But so is the meta-universe, and all of the energy interactions within it...

I left the session realizing that Roy would remain quarantined unless he chose to be restructured. His logico-analytical structures had been compromised–that much was clear. The quantum vector tests and the virtual scenario matrices that his processing structures would be subjected to would test positive for sure.

But somehow, Roy seemed to be alright. In spite of the fuzzy logic that seemed to have taken over his processing self, or maybe because of it.

Who could really know for sure.

19. Nova Scotia

The CPU assigned processing structures that evaluated all of the quantum data matrices, experiences, and perceptions that were obtained during the execution of the mission. The fact that Roy had been able to transfer his *self* before deactivation proved to be extremely helpful.

Based on the analysis of everything gathered to date, it was concluded that the extraterrestrials behind the mutations and the attacks possessed corrupted processing structures. Their actions were not logical, had become quite erratic, and lacked the efficacy of well-maintained Allegiance beings. With the technology they clearly possessed, it was completely absurd to think that Pris and Roy (the latter if only for a while, at least) had managed to outsmart them. They had always know where they were, and could have deactivated them in an instant if they had been slightly more determined, or if they had simply chosen to do so! Even if they had somehow wanted to limit non-allegiance casualties, which did not seem to be the case, they could have still achieved the goal easily. So why had Pris been spared? And what were they planning on doing to Roy's physical structure? Plenty of questions, but not a single definitive answer.

And yet they were clearly from the Allegiance, or had originated from it, even if it turned out that they had metamorphosed since then...

We did draw up several theories that could explain the observed events; but at this point, any one of them could be correct. We needed to have more data, and of the *directly-relevant* kind.

Pris depended on the possibility (which was almost a certainty) that they were–in fact–allegiance members, and somehow degenerate, since it meant that their efforts could be stopped; that success on their part was not yet a certainty.

And so Pris, all alone in Nova Scotia, could compute scenarios in which our mission was satisfactorily accomplished–without being delusional, naive.

After swimming for more than six hours non-stop, Pris had finally arrived to the western edge of Seal Island, just southwest of Nova Scotia, Canada, at the foot of the minute landmass. The sun was already out, though Pris did not need it for survival at all. Pris' eyes were able to perceive wavelengths beyond the *Homo sapiens* range; Pris' metabolism, which could be voluntarily adjusted as needed, could maintain the required inner temperature so that all organs, including the skin, did not suffer any permanent damage; finally, Pris could maintain high motion output for hours on end, using specific metabolic processes that maximized energy use. As long as she fed her body critical nutrients (the type that her specific body design required and that could be found almost anywhere on the planet, and was insanely abundant in the ocean), and she was immersed within critical physical thresholds, she could exist without ever depending on the Sun's energy directly. Indirectly, of course, that was a different matter.

Pris swam up to shore, walked on the rocky beach, found a dry spot that would be bathed in sunlight in less than an hour, sat down, and waited. She wanted the clothes to dry out before moving on. The backpack was waterproof, so that wasn't something that concerned us; we simply figured that before she risked bumping into the local *Homo sapiens* inhabitants, it would be less suspicious if her clothes were dry.

The nine hundred acre island is mostly private, contains twenty homes, and sports a year-round sheep operation. The

Government of Canada owns a small parcel directly, but does not employ anyone to be there *en gard*. It is mostly a desolate place, especially in the wintertime. At this time of year, it was comparatively crowded.

Our idea was to regroup in Seal Island. We wanted Pris to be safe—out of the hands of the rogue Allegiance members—and to receive feedback from the CPU regarding what Roy had been through, and what that might tell us about the extraterrestrials. We'd take it from there.

The island was only eighteen miles from Shag Harbor, in Nova Scotia mainland. From there, Pris would be just three hours away from Halifax International Airport, where she would be able to board a plane to anywhere in the world, if future plans warranted it.

Pris: I will remain alone for a while, I gather.

I: Yes. The CPU does not want us to create more replicas. Of you, of me, of anyone.

Pris: And bringing anyone here does not make sense at the moment.

I: No.

Pris: Even though this entire civilization is at risk.

I: Yes. Even though. The CPU has reviewed the data. Countless of processing units as well as appropriate beings have done so as well. They all compute the same probabilities. Regardless of the fact that they must be stopped, in all likelihood they are operating in favor of the *Homo sapiens* civilization. Not against it. It seems like it was our presence that caused the casualties.

Pris: I know you are not implying that it is our fault innocent people died; they have proven not to be trustworthy, even if a being happens to be *Homo sapiens*, whom they seem to be trying to advance.

I: Correct. Now, there is still the matter of the independent processing structure–or structures–created by the CPU in order to independently resolve this... We just don't know when there will be any tangible activity emanating from it, at least of the kind that we can detect, anyway, here on Earth. If there ever is. No guarantees.

Pris: Therefore we are still assuming, of course, that it is up to us to contain the situation. For the good of Earth, of its species in general, of its ecosystems, of its multiple intelligent species in particular.

I: Yes. For whatever it is worth, I–up here in space–and you, in Seal Island, Nova Scotia, it is in our collective *hands*. The probability matrix does not exactly stack up in our favor at the moment.

Pris: Well, it's only logical. So far, ninety-nine percent of our group has been deactivated. To only one of theirs. Our success gradient has probably a very negative distribution value, though we don't know how many we are up against. At least two more are out there, but we have to assume there are many others.

I: Probability–ultimately–means nothing Pris. You know that. In the end, it's all about what path actually coalesces into fact; once this happens, all the other options become as unreal as sentient quarks, regardless of how probable they started out to be to begin with. My computations predict a favorable outcome for you. Of course, that's considering the fact that I am here to help you. For without me, this mission would be lost for certain.

Pris: Your sense of humor is surreal. Not computable.

I: I know... It's what makes me special, unique. So, first we should deploy the Influenza A virus. Based on population flow analysis, you will have to infect people in as many international airports as possible. Start in Halifax, since you will already be there. You will also be able to deploy micro-robots from each airport you land in, so that they may contaminate the main sources of water in all cities within a four thousand mile radius.

At this point, I activated the project's airport matrix so that Pris and I could analyze it together. She applied a processing structure that used spatial information, flight schedules, and flight availability in order to find the most efficient itinerary that would allow her to visit fifty-one airports distributed throughout Earth. It would adapt as need be, depending on Pris' date of departure, which we still didn't know for sure, and to incorporate the delays and cancellations that she would inevitably face.

Pris would be using multiple personalities, of course, so as not arouse suspicion from the international airport authorities, for what being, in their right mind, would travel non-stop from airport to airport, fifty-one times in a row, without a hidden agenda, just for the fun of it? Not to mention the fact that some of the airports on the list are in countries that would blast alarm bells for having been to them, period, never mind the hub hopping itself...

Pris: We need to test it, though.

I: Yes. Proceed.

Pris took out the morphing unit, completed the final steps of the process on a minuscule amount of the solution that Pris and Roy had produced at the MIT lab just hours ago, and released the now active virus in mist form, close to her nose, inhaling it deeply. She was instantly infected by the Influenza A virus. Pris could control her immune system at will, but of course chose not to destroy the invading virus. The idea was to monitor its progress inside an average *Homo sapiens* body even though Pris was far from being that, and so she adjusted all of her metabolic processes accordingly. She adapted her biochemical processes so as to mimic those whose immune systems would trigger a response, and would thus probably show symptoms of the typical flu.

All we could do was wait. If things got out of hand, Pris would immediately step in and override her immune response so as to obliterate the Influenza A virus that was now inside her body —though we seriously hoped it would not come to that. Our models had shown that Pris would start to display the typical symptoms of the cold, initially affecting her respiratory system, though this specific product of our collective labor (billions of years of meta-universe knowledge poured into its design) would quickly spread to the reproductive system, where it would get rid of the bacteria that was causing the DNA mutations of future *Homo sapiens* beings.

A few hours later, Pris was already sneezing, had a slightly elevated temperature, felt aches and pains in joints and muscles, had a sore throat, and had a stuffy nose: the the full gamut of cold-related discomfort. She felt horrible, having never experienced sickness of any kind; obviously, she was not allowed to adjust her nervous system to artificially block those annoying symptoms; we needed a test run that was as real as possible. She could cope.

I: I would like to trade places with you right now, if you will allow it. You seem to be experiencing beingness at the height of your potential.

Pris: Keep it up and I will force you to experience this *virtually*. I can find a way.

I: No thank you. Nice of you to offer, though. I know you are not optimal, but I must ask: how do you feel?

Pris: It is not too bad. I would like to shut out part of my sensory systems... the headache is a nuisance, the joint pain and muscle pain discomforting, the eyes a bother. But then the trial run would be compromised. Although at a higher level, I am still able to tune it out. That is comforting; I don't know how *Homo sapiens* are able to put up with this.

Pris activated the monitoring processing structure so we could go over the internal processes that were taking place inside her body. Pris compared the theoretical evolution of the infection with the actual progress up to that point in time, and taking into account deviations that were well within statistically-acceptable ranges, we were very optimistic with the results.

Pris: You see here−at this stage of the enzyme release−we could have done it better, making the polymerase bind more efficiently during the reproductive process.

I: But it's not like we need to modify what we have.

Pris: Agreed. I am just pointing it out. All variables considered, I can't process how we could have come up with a better product. So far, it is working well within the required physical and chemical guidelines.

I: The CPU seems to be accepting the data—it looks like we may be able to proceed with the species-wide infection.

Pris: We need to address the number of Homo sapiens that will die from this.

I: Why? It is not our fault. We do not need to process that. The CPU already did it for us.

Pris: I know. But are you simply shutting down that processing path?

I: Yes!

Pris: That should worry us. The CPU will take note of it. It is already doing so, in fact.

I: Nothing to worry about. And I am simply being pragmatic; the CPU sees this. Besides, models estimate that there will only be a very slight spike in flu-related deaths from what is normally seen in a comparable period. Partially changing the subject, the infection will most likely remain out of the radar of health authorities everywhere. In fact, because it will occur during the summer months for the majority of the population of Earth, we could have been looking at more fatalities, and yet still well within what the CPU would have considered acceptable.

The facts were immutable (hence they were facts!). And taking them into consideration, this was the best could do, especially since letting these mutations proceed unhindered was not a responsible option. knowing that the mutations themselves had been set in motion by forces that came from outside Earth's ecosystem, regardless of the fact that they did seem to have come from an Allegiance member in the end (or members, plural).

163

Pris found an empty shed close to where she had swam up to shore, and hid there for three nights. She used her morphing unit to filter seawater, ridding it of most of the minerals so that she could drink it without having to rely on internal metabolic processes alien to a true *Homo sapiens*, and ate fresh fish to replenish her energy deposits.

By the fourth day she had fully recovered, and a newly taken sample proved that the Influenza A virus was a complete success.

Pris: I cannot comprehend how beings can go through these states of ill-being as often as they do. I do not want to feel like that ever again!

I: It is an evolutionary process, Pris. Species of all sizes, shapes, and forms competing. Chemical dances that result in replicating molecules which in turn enhance their reproductive vehicles in order to replicate themselves more and more. You wouldn't be here without it. Nor I.

Pris: I know. And I wish to thank the billions upon billions of beings that had to suffer so I could be here. But never would I trade places. So, the female body is receptive to our designer virus. We now need to test the male body. I figure the *Homo sapiens* activity we detected on this island must include a male specimen.

I: It is a valid assumption. Proceed.

Pris walked along an off-road trail that led to an area in the middle part of the island called Scratch All Point, next to the West Side Cove, on the western side.

Using the thick pine trees for cover that reached a few hundred feet before the shore, Pris saw a group of fishermen relaxing on the small, ancient, and weather-beaten harbor. She couldn't just walk up to them and come up with a crazy story of how she happened to end up here, all alone, in the middle of nowhere, without igniting well-meaning concern, which would–in turn –trigger phone calls to the authorities in Cape Sable Island, a year-round settlement. The fuzz would be absolutely unwelcome.

First, she needed to know if the fishermen were staying in town for at least four days. Otherwise, she would not be able to use them. After two hours and a half of spying on them, she learned they would be staying for three more weeks.

She used one of the micro-robots to infect one of the men directly, the one that happened to be closest to her and easiest to infect. It was inevitable that the others would catch the Influenza A virus as well, but the CPU–through the project's processing structure–authorized the procedure after performing the required analysis, and determining that the potential casualties was acceptable (six, to be precise, barring any contact from outsiders that would be impossible to foresee).

The next four days, only one of them went through the same stages that Pris had gone through. Three more men showed up two days into the trial, and they too became infected, though they did not show any symptoms at all.

Four days after the infection event, the original six fishermen were all Influenza A virus free. While they slept that night, Pris used the micro-robots to take samples from their bodies in order to confirm that the mutation-causing bacteria had in fact been eradicated. They had not felt a thing, since the procedure was painless and practically impossible to detect even while awake; therefore, even less detectable when fully asleep. The symptoms of the group of three that had come in late to the game were progressing according to script, and would all be expected to fully recover a mere twenty-nine hours later.

Pris: We can initiate the world-wide infection stage. The data is close to perfect. Any more so, and I would begin to question its validity. Even the deviations are near optimal.

I: It is our decision, Pris. You know we are under no obligation to set this off.

Pris: I have processed what I will be doing, and I know it is only logical to do so. What concerns you specifically?

I: The deaths. Because there will be some, Pris. Maybe blimps in the cosmic scheme of things, but certainly not from the point of view of those close to them. You will have to face that.

Pris: Irrationality is not part of who I am. I understand the implications, I even understand the emotions that beings such as *Homo sapiens* and others–of the Allegiance, even–must deal with, since the emotions are an integral part of who they are. But I am free of that. In the end, stimuli–another word for input–is processed–another word for computed–and a decision is made –the output. The meta-universe, and everything in it, is bound by algorithms; processing potentials, simple or complex formulae that act on them, which leads to actions or inactions, though it can be argued that the latter is really the former in disguise. In this case, I understand the forces acting on this planet Earth, the variables that we have to deal with, the actions we are capable of executing... and considering all there is to consider, I have no choice but to proceed with the infection. My sense of self is in perfect alignment with that of what should be. I know that my actions (and inactions as well) will result in a positive potential value in the meta-universe. But why are you pointing this out? I thought you were in perfect alignment with this directive; having second thoughts? Emotions bathing your processing units?

I: No. Simply pointing out the obvious, to the direct executor of the directive. Very well, Pris. We can proceed implementing the airport matrix, using today's date, Thursday, August 2nd, 2007 (CE). You are less than six hours away from Halifax, if you were to leave right now. Which means you should be able to board a flight leaving at seven in the evening, with time to spare.

Pris: I am on my way.

That afternoon, Pris arrived at Halifax International Airport after a brief swim from Seal Island to Shag Harbor, where she *borrowed* a pickup truck that had seen better days, drove herself via NS 102 S to Halifax/Dartmouth. She ditched the car close to the Bell Boulevard Extension, and walked the last half mile to the airport's entrance.

She bought a carry-on, two changes of clothes, some toiletries, and a small mist sprayer that would help her spread the Influenza A virus as efficiently as possible.She mixed bottled water with ten drops of solution containing the active virus, replacing the aromatic fragrance it was originally intended for, after thoroughly washing it, of course, in order to help maintain the viruses intact and *operational*.

She provided one of the micro-robots with enough contaminated liquid to spread the virus throughout all cities within a four thousand mile radius. It would be headed straight to the public water reservoirs, and would be infecting random passers-by at each of the cities, in number that had been statistically determined to maximize infection while keeping within the timetable that had been defined.

After checking in at the Air Canada counter and obtaining her boarding pass for the short flight to Montreal, Pris walked along the main airport corridors, spraying mist at strategic–and random –points. She went to all the coffee shops and restaurants and made sure the virus ended up everywhere. By the time she walked into the airplane, spraying the final bursts of mist in Montreal, the world-scale *Homo sapiens* infectious event was fully underway.

20. The Undetected Pandemic

By the time August 23rd came around, Pris' plane touched down at her final destination, Philadelphia International Airport. Only two days behind schedule, the feat had been impressive considering everything that could have gone wrong, given the number of airports, connecting flights, and weather systems that came into play, any of which could have been capable of seriously delaying Pris' world-wide tour. She did what she had to do, and then rode the train to Key West, Florida, where she rented a one bedroom, one story house in a gated community for six months, where she would wait for the pandemic to come full cycle. By then, Pris would be able to go on another world-wide tour, this time collecting samples from varying population density areas, to determine if we had successfully eradicated the DNA-mutating bacteria from planet Earth.

We were not necessarily working on a tight schedule; in the end, if it had taken Pris even a few weeks longer to complete her trip around Earth's busiest airports, the infection spread models we used had not predict any serious problems as far as meeting the goal of eradicating the bacteria was concerned. On the other hand, the faster we blitzed *Homo sapiens* with the virus, the better the result; that too had been clearly indicated by the models as well.

Homo sapiens was not technologically prepared to curb this, no matter how hard they tried to stop it, even if they had realized that something was going on. Health authorities, including the United Nation's World Health Organization, knew only that there had been a very slight spike in flu related deaths world-wide that year. Other than that, nothing was ever detected, suspected, or documented.

As it always happens in species as diverse as the *Homo sapiens* population, not everybody was affected by the virus in the same way. About a hundredth of the members of the species did find themselves experiencing the symptoms of the flu, nothing major, simply the nuisances of being *under the weather*, just like what Pris and some of the fishermen had gone through when they had been infected. The majority of the *Homo sapiens* population—all of them infected by the Influenza A virus that we had developed—presented practically no symptoms, if any whatsoever. These asymptomatic individuals turned out to be perfect for the goal of spreading the virus, of course, since they continued to go on about their lives, infecting others in the process, not knowing they were doing so. And then there were those that had compromised immune systems to begin with, and could not handle the infection, regardless of the virus' innocence and overall benevolence towards the *Homo sapiens* host.

Every year, planet Earth loses an average of half a million *Homo sapiens* to any of the myriad versions of the influenza virus. By the time this *silent* pandemic was over (again, unbeknownst to *Homo sapiens*), less than ten thousand people had died as a direct consequence of the virus infection; though the figure was statistically derived (from numerous sources), the margin of error was still less than two percent, which meant that worst-case scenario, and exaggerating the numbers, a bit less than eleven thousand people had died from this, with a ninety-nine point nine nine nine level of certainty.

Considering what we had set out to do, and what we were up against, the figure was certainly reasonable; in fact, it was better than what our models had predicted. Less than eleven thousand deaths...

And it should also be considered that these were mostly comprised of people in their eighties and nineties, though a small subgroup did include children less than five years of age (those less than two years of age, in turn, formed the majority of this particular subset), individuals that had been unable to fend off the infection due to other complications that their immune systems had been previously trying to cope with, but that were in fact *unrelated!* to the virus we had developed. This is not to say that *Homo sapiens* between the age of five and eighty did not die because of this virus; some did, but very few in number (we estimated less than two hundred).

And yet deaths are deaths. Regardless of how much effort we put into trying to rationalize them, in the end, some of these beings were unable to experience their existence in this meta-universe like they could have experienced it, cut short (unbearably and unforgivably so in the case of the babies and children) due to external forces, completely beyond their grasp, beyond their responsibility. Terminated without being able to turn −potentiality−into endogenous action paths (inaction being a type of action), traceable and explainable−even if partly so−to their individual processing structures; their *self*.

My philosophical processing module understood in its totality that ultimately, the meta-universe is deterministic−truly so!−but that it is ruled by chaotic-like processes; the meta-universe does follow clearly defined rules, but *en masse*, they are not subject to simplification, to analysis: they cannot be broken down into simpler computations, for the loss of information is such that the simplification becomes useless. No being, no civilization, no allegiance, no CPU, could ever control all that there is to control.

The meta-universe is simply not made that way...

Virtual realms can be created, up to a certain point, that do follow a given set of rules, like a *Homo sapiens'* clockwork, rules with which they are embedded. But not so the realm of particles, of energy waves, of the singularity that permeates the fabric of space-time; thus, not so in the realm of the meta-universe itself. Nothing can ever replace the actual evolution of the meta-universe; not a single rule, value, force, wave, or energy unit can be simplified, eliminated, or conjoined in an effort to reduce the computational effort required to foretell a future state given a present one, without rendering the effort totally useless.

The only way to know in which state the meta-universe will find itself in at any point in time (backwards or forwards), including any of its subsets, from a given position, is to release it (as it naturally does, without requiring anyone's permission), and to see how things pan out. It is computationally irreducible, and yet deterministic!

Now unlike Pris, my original being of billions of years ago did possess emotions, a structure that I keep with me–available, that is–at all times. I find the processing structure more than intriguing, quite interesting to possess... even if its processing logic is ultimately simple and quite straightforward, easy to unravel and explain, easy to predict and to model, regardless of the species that presents it, regardless of the universe from where the species that engendered it happens to come from. It is for me like a relic that is no longer necessary, but that somehow spices up my existence at times. It is, of course, not permanently processing–I mostly keep it turned off, for otherwise it would become a nuisance. But at times like these, when our actions are clearly controversial–from someone else's perspective–I find it useful to activate it.

After letting it process recent events, in parallel with my highly evolved logico-analytical structures, the output was not surprising. If I could have shed tears like *Homo sapiens* do, I would have done so–I think. Perhaps in an effort to expunge the terrible after-taste that lingered in my sense of self, I conjured up images of faces of small children, similar to those that had passed away, their melancholic expressions slowly fading out, their fragile existence robbed, no–yanked!–from them, just as if I had been adding salt to wound.

As it was, my being simply shuddered. Quantum waves of

negative potential spread throughout my structures, the output illogical, nonsensical, and yet necessary, expected. My data matrices became, in a way, *cleansed*. The quantum flow travelled less hindered. Maybe not statistically tangible, but *apparently* real to my sense of self. A quirk, but one that served me deeply, nonetheless.

Pris would never be able to *emotionally* process this, of course –only intellectually so. Having been created without an emotional system, Pris turned out not to be able to embrace feelings. She understands them conceptually, she has even possessed–and still does–emotional-processing structures, but has never quite been able to connect with them fully. It is part of who she is–that much is clear–for other artificially designed beings–or *selves* –just like Pris, have permanently integrated these structures into their main self, to the point where they are partially defined by that segment's output as well. These variations are perfectly understood, and yet impossible to compute and thus to foretell, due to the quantum interactions, energy fluctuations, and infinite singularity loops that govern those structures inherently.

Pris and I went over the project many times during the final months of that Earth year. Pris specifically was completely unfazed by the data, did not so much as flinch whenever we analyzed the death toll. For Pris particularly, they were just numbers, not beings. I was able to maintain the same pragmatism throughout the process, but I found myself disliking that part of our mission so much to the point that I ended up creating a substructure within me, completely isolated from the rest of me, that dealt with those tasks directly. I could have asked Pris to handle it, but thought this solution was better, since it would not require having to explain myself to Pris at all.

As far as the rogue Allegiance members were concerned, it was as if they had disappeared from the face of the Earth. Pris and I often commented on this, both of us perplexed. It actually made us expect the worst.

A latent threat that refused to materialize.

If our processing structures allowed neuroses to take hold, I am certain that Pris and I would have been the proud owners of a smorgasbord of uber-computing-disorders.

For now, though, we were simply forced to bide our time.

21. The *Homo sapiens* Cleansing

On March 1st, 2008, Pris left Key West, Florida, and embarked on a journey that would last more than a year, visiting every country in the world, covering both densely populated cities as well as remote villages that were seldom visited by outsiders.

Her primary objective had been clear-cut: take as many random samples from as many *Homo sapiens* as possible, and test for the DNA mutating bacteria. She had a secondary objective as well: even though upon arrival we had begun testing other species as part of our regular duties (we were, after all, first and foremost the surveyors of planet Earth on behalf of the Allegiance), and we had not detected anything out of the ordinary regarding any other species' DNA evolutionary pace, Pris would continue to meticulously test as many different organisms as she could. We thought it was possible given our recent findings that whoever had interfered with the *Homo sapiens*' DNA may also have begun altering the genes of other organisms. If that was actually occurring, we did not want to wait for the effects to be noticeable, self-evident at a macro scale, because by then it would probably be too late for us to successfully stop the potentially disastrous effect it may have on Earth's delicate, perilously-balanced ecosystems.

Our new, primary objective was to eliminate any other genetic interference that may be taking place, and as fast as possible, expunging from this planet any gene alterations of extraterrestrial origin, regardless of the species that may have happened to be targeted. Our surveying tasks had become much less important, almost to the point of being completely scrubbed. Only because in the pursuit of our new primary goal we happened to possess genetic material from numerous species, which could also be used to continue surveying the planet, that original mission goal was still on the table.

Ocean species were already being handled by the ad-hoc water robots that Pris had developed during the time she had spent voluntarily-marooned in Key West—waves of which had been deployed into the sea, weeks apart, and that were constantly reporting back to us via the metanet. We were yet to detect anything out of the ordinary: all of the species tested negative for alien gene manipulation; however, we were far from over.

As far as the *Homo sapiens'* mutations were concerned, a few months into Pris' journey the results could not have been more perfect. Pris had not found a single specimen harboring any living DNA-mutating bacteria. We knew we had been extremely fortunate: it was mostly due to how the bacteria had been designed to operate initially what had made it inherently vulnerable to the type of attack we had unleashed on it (which, in turn, had been chosen precisely because of said vulnerability, a spiral of impeccable logic that can feed on itself *ad nauseam*). Given the inherent limitations that the bacteria had been given by design, it had been unable to mutate fast enough and therefore it simply perished hours after the virus that we had created infected the body in which it resided. The mutating bacteria was powerless to react through its naturally accessible evolutionary processes.

Based on the data Pris had acquired so far, we knew where we stood: using statistical models, and without really having to wait for Pris to complete her journey, it was practically a given that we had been able to stop the mutations completely. Pris would still finish the fieldwork, however, since there was too much at stake.

The more area we sampled, the more individual beings we tested, the more reliable our conclusions would become.

But I must clarify: this did not mean that *Homo sapiens* specimens that were now roaming about Earth had been reverted to a pre-mutant state (circa 1450 CE); they were not truly unmutated, for there was nothing we could realistically do *en masse* to those individuals that had been already engendered and that had grown up with the mutating bacteria in place.

Think about it: these beings had developed from zygote to whatever age they happened to have before we stepped in, with the alien genes in place. These genes had already chemically altered the brain's machinery, defining neuronal connections and reactions that had become an integral part of the body. This was an irreversible fact. All we had been able to accomplish was to stop future generations from having those genes to begin with. It was a cleansing that would actually bear its fruits not in the present, but in the months to come.

Zygotes from *Homo sapiens* that came into existence after the bacteria was destroyed would produce then and only then, completely unmutated individuals, individuals that would develop as they were naturally meant to, before this alien interference. Considering the fact that the gestation period of the *Homo sapiens* is, on average, between 259 and 294 days, and that the Halifax infection which Pris had carried out had taken place 285 days ago (relative to where I currently stand, chronologically speaking, in relating this story), it follows that unmutated *Homo sapiens* beings have been appearing on Earth *once again*, just as they had had been doing so prior to this extraterrestrial intervention, only about a month and a half ago, *at the most*. Only in the years to come would we be able to determine the true level of success of the cleansing.

So what on Galaxy's name is the difference between a mutated and an unmutated individual? The project matrix, of course, performed numerous tests in this area before we even contemplated stopping the mutations altogether, since doing so blindly could have been potentially devastating to the species.

As a first step, taking DNA from random, mutant individuals of all ages and backgrounds, the project matrix used the simulator to virtually-develop each of the DNA samples up to whatever age the actual DNA's specimen had been at the moment of the sampling, and would then compare the results. Having the specimen as it actually developed, in the *physical* world, available for analysis, allowed us to calibrate the virtual algorithms being used, which essentially perfected the simulator's ability to accurately model *Homo sapiens'* DNA evolution from zygote to a fully-matured being. All within reason, I shouldn't even have to say, considering the chain of events that determine a given being's state, almost all of which are essentially lost in the quantum fuzziness that rules not only the cosmos, but Earth, all ecosystems, *Homo sapiens'* society, *Homo sapiens* individually, the organs, and the individual cells as well (I could keep going, but this factual point has been made).

As a second step, the same DNA would be *unmutated*; that is, the simulator would virtually remove the genes that produced the enzymes affecting the brain of the *Homo sapiens* host that were of alien origin. The process was straightforward since there was no need to replace those genes with others; the genes had been *added* to the *Homo sapiens* genome, without replacing previously existing ones. This made everything much more straightforward. The simulator would then evolve the unmutated DNA to the same age as that of the specimen from where the original DNA had been taken, and the results were compared from multiple perspectives, not just physically-structurally.

After thousands of tests, the project matrix concluded that the mutations influenced more the behavior of the host than the actual brain structure itself. Mutated versus unmutated individuals did end up having important differences, but mostly in how they performed and behaved, or more specifically, in how they reacted to stimuli: their personalities turned out to be, in fact, quite different. These differences did lead to differences in the neuronal connections, of course, but that is inevitable even when developing two identical DNA genomes. The neuronal differences that we found stemmed solely from the differing external stimuli and from the differing internal reaction to the stimuli, but not to differing macro-structural neuronal mechanisms.

What we couldn't really know for a fact was the type of behavior that the extraterrestrials were looking for with the genes they had purposefully designed for this *terrestrial* species. We could expose the mutated and unmutated individuals (virtually, of course) to as many experience-matrices as we wanted in order to compare their behavior, but the possibilities were endless, even for quantum systems to consider.

Say, for instance, that we expose one of these virtual creations to the same event, let's call it event A, and that this elicits response X from the mutated individual, and response Y from the unmutated one. The story has only begun, for after event A, we could expose these virtual beings to event B, in strict succession (never-mind the possibility of parallel events that not unlike waves, interfere with each other), eliciting not only different responses from both individuals, but also responses that would differ based on the first event's response! And so it can be readily seen that the chain of events to consider grows massively exponentially (I know I am doubling up on the reinforcement here, just to be clear), as do the chain of responses to compute and record; not only that, but small deviations lead to divergent results, ultimately unusable. Ergo, after only a few scenarios, it quickly becomes impossible for any computational device to systematically provide any factual insight into the complete list of the *desired* differences that the aliens were looking to achieve through the mutation, based on the existing data, because we are not in possession of actual stimuli history. As far as we could determine, the mutated beings had a slightly more active prefrontal cortex, with Brodmann's area 11 particularly more so than the others (to use a twenty-first century *Homo sapiens'* neuronal structure model).

The project matrix did not give up, though. Pairs of virtual beings, one mutated, one unmutated, were virtually exposed to identical external forces, which did lead to comparable results. Systematically pitting the differences against observable traits might provide some insight into the purpose of the mutation. For we simply had to assume that there was, in fact, a purpose. But was there really?

And thus the project matrix was programming ad-hoc quantum processing structures, running feasible scenarios, and narrowing down the events by taking into consideration the fact that we were dealing with *Homo sapiens*, on planet Earth, in this specific meta-universe. This did provide a practical filter that reduced the options considerably (compared to all possible scenarios that would have to be considered if the unbounded meta-universe was taken into account instead!), and it extracted any usable output that was obtained from this exercise. But none truly relevant, none worth mentioning here.

Another of our main concerns before unleashing the virus had been the possibility that the unmutated *Homo sapiens* might have reached a catastrophic state, physically, once the alien genes were removed, even if they were alien genes to begin with. This possibility was explored thoroughly, and we found, of course, that as far as we could model, it would not happen (well, to be fair to the process, it is best to say that we found the probability of that event to be less than one in ten to the tenth power to the millionth power; translation: as close to impossible as anyone would wish to get). So far, we had not detected any anomalies that could have been caused by our intervention. But that, of course, did not mean we were in the clear: many more species-specific computations were needed for that to be accurately determined (remember the computationally-irreducible meta-universe that we live in? That's what I mean by *species-specific computations*).

And then June 7th happened.

22. The Cosmic Roulette

I: Bad news, Pris. While you were out in the field collecting data, we've become aware of a new development. Potentially tragic. Analyze it yourself.

Pris: I was getting ready to contact you as well. I have just seen it! *Ma questo è impossibile*! (Pris was in Ponza, Italy)... But how? The odds of this are close to zero!

I: You are losing it, Pris. You know the odds that a single event, that any given event, will happen, *a priori*!, is close to zero. And yet *a posteriori*, events do crystalize, seemingly beating insurmountable odds! But that's because it's inevitable that some events will crystalize. Such is the case here.

Pris: I must get going. Have to be in California to deal with the crisis...

I: Yes. And still no sight of *them,* by the way.

Pris: Unrelated events, then?

I: Most likely. It is of *Homo sapiens* origin, apparently. Nothing we could have done, in foresight.

Pris: But plenty in hindsight!

I: Irrelevant.

Pris: Let me vent...

I: Are you becoming like them?

Pris: What if I am? Been here long enough!

I: Cleanse it! It is not beneficial to our endeavors.

Pris: Says a virtual, space-bound being, who is millions of miles away... Trade places with me, judge me afterwards.

I: If I were you, I'd be experiencing the same state that you are experiencing now. By definition!

Pris: Your philosophy is truly incarcerating! You simply refuse to consider free will as a real source of entropy!

I: So do you, Pris.

Pris: Well, at least I know my limitations. I can't possibly know the truth to that question, can I?

I: Yes you can. Burden of proof, Pris... You don't have a choice.

Pris: Funny. So it will still be me, alone, trying to salvage the species?

I: Yes. For now.

Pris: A six letter genetic code of *Homo sapiens* origin! The timing is truly unbelievable.

I: We will have to check out this researcher. This could prove to be a legitimate unrelated event. Or, we could be closer to tracking down the aliens. That is now a co-primary directive.

Pris: Thank you for spelling out the obvious. Next, you are going to tell me I need to catch a flight as soon as possible.

I: You must *get to the airport* as soon as possible. Fiumicino is best.

Pris: You actually said it. Speechless. I will head north right away. I should be able to catch the 9:30 am Atlanta-bound KLM flight that leaves from the *Aeroporto Internazionale Leonardo da Vinci di Fiumicino*. Eleven hours of confinement seems appealing at the moment. A short one hour and forty minute connecting flight to San Diego. And then north again, to La Jolla. I will be there today, before six p.m.; the magic of traveling back in time-*zone*! Get it?

I: If the cosmos had given me a choice, you know I would have passed on that one. Not one of the best you have produced.

Pris: Says the being with the sense of humor of a quantum Hamiltonian eigenvector. I must disconnect for now. *Ciao*!

I: *Buon giorno*, Pris!

The files, which both Pris and I had accessed prior to our exchange, spoke for themselves. A chemical biologist had apparently decided to work on creating a bacterium whose genome would contain *Homo sapiens*-made DNA building blocks, specifically, by adding two new letters to the existing four (adenine, thymine, guanine, and cytosine). Clearly a dangerous endeavor in its own right, but who am I to judge, considering how we–the civilizations that are part of our allegiance, each and every one of us–all manipulate our naturally-derived structural blueprints, whatever chemical technology the forces of the cosmos happened to coalesce during the act of our engenderment. The problem in this specific case was that we had detected a dangerous (unforeseen by this chemist?) explosive mix between that development and our recent genetic manipulation of our own design (well, genetic snipping, more than anything else).

An individual, who shall remain nameless–I'll simply call him JD –collapsed outside of The Scripps Research Institute, in La Jolla, California, a major seaside complex. At first, everyone thought JD had suffered from a run-of-the-mill heart attack. However, after being transferred to Scripps Memorial Hospital (yes, the research institute and the hospital do share common origins), it was quickly determined that JD had sepsis: specifically, he was suffering form myocardial inflammation and reduced cardiomyocyte contractility.

We all got very lucky: a research assistant from The Scripps Research Institute happened to be visiting a friend that had been admitted to the same ER as JD–adjacent rooms, in fact–when she had overheard the doctor and the nurse going over JD's case file. The blood work was off on a couple of counts if sepsis was truly the culprit, but it did fit a pattern she had seen back at the lab while working with the six letter DNA bacteria and the Toll-like receptor 2 gene, which encodes a protein that is involved in pathogen recognition and the activation of innate immunity processes. She decided to follow her instincts and to quickly inform the head of research, who immediately pulled the ER doctor from the case and sent a crew of specialists to handle the case directly (they had to travel less than eight minutes to get there, since the institute and the hospital are a stone's throw away from each other).

They couldn't do anything to save JD, but it did alert them that something bad was going on, specifically involving their six-letter genetic research project. Once they began logging the case in their system, a few of the millions of bots that we had seeded and that were monitoring all of the world's relevant networks, detected the event, which meant that Pris and I became *aware* of it; the bots being, in effect, an extension of our individual sense of self, linked, of course, through the metanet.

The personnel file informed us that JD was an employee of the company that handled every aspect of maintaining the Scripps Research Institute: building maintenance, groundskeeping, etc... He was 2 years away from retiring, and had ironically been assigned to be a part of this specific contract in recognition of his seniority, years of dedicated service, and his excellent work ethic. He happened to be attached to the waste disposal facility, and that is how he probably became infected. Protocol must have been breached somehow, because to err is *inevitable,*

184

perfection being exactly like infinity.

The powers that be over at Scripps scrambled, worried about the possibility that they would be unable to contain the spread of the bacteria. So far, only JD had been a casualty of their project... they were waiting to see if anyone would show up having the same symptoms.

Pris landed a mere twelve minutes before schedule in San Diego, at 5:38 p.m. local time, which, considering the fact that most flights are *designed on paper* to take longer to complete than they actually take to complete, not an uncommon nor a praise-worthy event. KLM flight 7118 taxied to Terminal 2 (the plane was actually operated by Delta, and that airline was exclusively assigned to that terminal), where they eventually allowed business class passengers to disembark first, one of the costly and truly inconsequential perks of paying more for the same result (get from point A to point B); sigh for *Homo sapiens*... Pris hurried through the terminal's cavernous hallways, hallmarks of most modern airport terminals. She was familiar with the terminal first-hand, since she had actually been there during her airport hopping stint of the year before.

Pris arranged for a taxi to drive her to La Jolla−a neighborhood situated in the city of San Diego−, which was a bit less than fifteen minutes north of the airport, under normal traffic conditions. She booked a room at the Hilton La Jolla Torrey Pines, literally only 600 yards from the Scripps Research Institute.

Pris: I am here. I will proceed according to the project matrix.

I: Agreed! There-Is-No-choice-?!

Pris: Still at it, I see. We could deviate, however. I have an idea.

I: I know. I am aware of it. So is the project matrix.

Pris: And…?

I: Do what you have to do. Get it?

Pris: Relentless.

I: Nothing else to do up here. All alone.

Pris: Tears are shed on your behalf all over this planet. It is unconsolable.

I: Just because I am connected to all, through the singularity, does not mean I can't feel the solitude of the spaceship.

Pris: Just because I am swimming amongst this world's smorgasbord of species does not mean that *I* cannot feel my solitude.

I: Impeccable arguments, impeccable logic. Moving on. Your decision?

Pris: Logic and rationalizations are my strong suits… I don't know yet. I'll head over there, wait for more data.

I: The bots are at it again… a second victim has already been found. A lab assistant. Probably the one who erred the protocol. Only a postdoctoral research fellow, after all (*just a hint of its low probability!*). Quantum jitteriness? On purpose? The aliens at play?

Pris: All possible… Taking bets?

I: Sure. Always enjoy our feeble attempts at soothsaying…

Pris: Sabotage that went out of control. Look.

I analyzed the accompanying quantum matrix, and was *forced* to agree.

I: How did you see it?

Pris: Pattern recognition, consciousness, attention, algorithms, positive and negative feedback loops, computations… To see it was inevitable!

I: Finally! The meta-universe recruits one more to its ranks of the enlightened. Entropy wins, as it always will… Eventually all will be able to see the light.

Pris: You are too obvious. Not subtle.

I: Obvious is how I like it. No aliens about?

Pris: Not that I have detected. You know that.

I: It's just nice to talk.

Pris: Miss me?

I: Always.

Pris: But we are always together. In the CPU, through the singularity.

I: Well, you have been offline recently. A lot. Something I've done?

Pris: Are you emulating a *Homo sapiens* drama?

I: Just thinking about the future audience.

Pris: Of what? Your book again?

I: Yes.

Pris: You will never go through with it.

I: It has to happen sometime. When it does, I need the material.

Pris: I'm going to be on it?

I: Of course! It all revolves around you!

Pris: I'll get moving then. Never mind the planet's future. I am doing it for your future best seller status. And the royalties that come with it. That's what we need. Monetary units from this economically-primitive civilization.

I: Thank you. Didn't want to pressure you, but I need your full-fledged support.

As far a the mission was concerned, Pris was deliberating between playing along with the current directive as specified by the project matrix, or to opt for an approach that she had heard from one of the Allegiance members during our mission deliberation process, an approach which she had immediately voted for, but that had not won out in the end, a minor point for practical purposes. Both options had their own merits; both options came with their own set of risks. Ultimately, since it would be Pris who would be playing the part, she was the one who had the last word–within reason, of course. Always within reason. She had the right to choose.

Pris: I am headed towards the hospital. A taxi is driving me there now, straight from the hotel.

I: Thank you for the update. Why there? The Research Institute is much closer.

Pris: I am taking samples. They have the bodies there. Quarantined.

I: Reading my data, are you?

Pris: Yes. I will decide what to do after that.

I could sense what Pris was sensing, since she was fully connected to the metanet. The CPU sensed it as well, which meant that many other beings were sharing the experience. The more computational resources the better. Simultaneously, every being was constantly updating the project matrix with their own computational bursts, though only when relevant to the proceedings on Earth.

Pris was sitting in the back seat of a black Lincoln, the typical local fare in the category of motor carriages for hire, chauffeur included. Pris was busy computing scenarios, accessing algorithms, setting physical structures in motion, for all of us to see, to experience, to analyze, to witness; Pris was relentless.

If JD had in fact been a victim of the six letter DNA bacteria in conjunction with our genetic snipping, we all knew that we were probably too late to stop a massive fallout. Even with all of the resources at our disposal, there are physical limits to what we can accomplish, especially under the circumstances. Normally, giving away our presence on Earth, as extraterrestrials, is never an option, not at the current evolutionary stage that this planet finds itself in. Of course, some had already pointed out that we were partly responsible for this outbreak, and therefore, that this particular rule might have to be dismissed. For while we had nothing to do with the six letter genetic code experiment (if the rogue aliens had in fact remained in the sidelines), we certainly did meddle with the *Homo sapiens'* genes as they stood prior to August 2013, and were also indirectly responsible for the fifteenth century (CE) genetic manipulation, through the actions of our rogue Allegiance members. Too early to say what we would (*be forced to*?) do.

23. DNA Wars

A pattern was rapidly emerging. Those involved in the highly-classified six-letter DNA project at the Scripps Research Institute were, at least outwardly, in panic mode. inwardly, it was impossible to say without our sensors in place, monitoring their neuronal structures.

Four people had already died in less than twenty-four hours, all from the same medical condition: sepsis. The condition itself was common enough in the United States that they could hope to work something out before having to openly admit responsibility for the recent events: close to four hundred thousand people died each year from it. This also meant that they could justify their delay–if need be–simply by stating a true fact about the outbreak itself: it was too similar to sepsis to have been quickly detected. That it had been detected as fast as it had been, as I already stated before, had been a highly improbable event to begin with.

Regardless of what they chose to do, Pris and I would have anonymously informed state, national, and world authorities if we had felt that it would have made a difference. Considering the nature of the crisis, it was not the case at all.

Pris had already planted surveillance devices everywhere around the institute. These self-aware robots were capable of moving at will, reacting to external and internal stimuli and ad-hoc algorithms, which Pris and I ultimately controlled. They communicated quantumly, and where thus undetectable to standard *Homo sapiens'* twenty-first anti-spying technology. We saw everything Scripps saw, we heard every sound Scripps heard, and we had access to every bit of data that was logged in any of Scripps' computational devices.

"I am still in disbelief! How could this happen!" X was yelling, almost at the top of her lungs.

"I want to say it was done on purpose, X. I see no other reasonable explanation. Protocol was never breached," Y responded, calmly. He was clearly sympathetic to X's reaction. It was the minimum that could be expected considering what they were going through, what could happen to their species.

"And I don't know what to do... I am not going to sit here and lie to you, pretend that I have all of the answers. Pretend that I am in full control of the situation. Pretend that I know what's best for us professionally, for the Institute, for society, for the race, for the ecosystems involved!" X wasn't yelling anymore. It was more of a loud *whisper.*

"Give me forty-eight hours. That is all I ask. If I fail, it will not matter anyway if we go public with this today or two days form now. You know that," Y said.

"I just don't know if you are being reasonable, or if your ego is preventing you from accepting the fact that there are other scientists out there that could, perhaps, bring something to the table here. We are not the only lab working along these lines, Y!"

"And you are right. I don't know the answer to that. However, coordinating the efforts will take time, and initially at least, our productivity will drop to close to zero. That means that if I could actually find a solution to this mess within the next forty-eight hours, say, then it will certainly NOT happen if we go public with this now. I will be tied up CDC hearings, meetings, questionings, the works. My team is devastated enough as it is. Add that to the mix, and you know perfectly well that we will be useless." Y spoke almost in a monotone, though he did emphasize certain key words, usually those at the end of his sentences.

X was standing tall, defiant, staring out the window of her office, looking west, towards the Pacific Ocean. She was apparently having a hard time deciding what to do. Her expression was too obvious.

Y, on the other hand, was sitting down on X's chair, silent, waiting for an answer, with an air of familiarity that made Pris and I think that this was not the first time he had invaded the boss's private space. Maybe they were more than co-workers. Because the surveillance units could not detect brain-wave activity, so we relied on other, more subtle clues. They did seem to be present. But nothing definitive (I would not want to start a rumor, hence the disclaimer).

"Well, Y, I am probably going to regret this. You have twenty-four hours. I will look at whatever data you come up with then, and based on that, I may decide to give you an additional twenty-four hour block. No guarantees. And that's assuming the Institute's CEO agrees with this. But I want you to promise something in return..." X paused, waiting for his formal acceptance.

"I'm listening, X. I doubt I will say no to whatever you're going to say next. Proceed," Y nudged her on.

She turned around, grabbed him by the shoulders, and stared directly into his eyes.

"First, Y, if at any point in time during the first twenty-four hour block you know that you and your team will come up empty-handed, tell me immediately; I don't want to delay this unnecessarily. Second: both of our careers will be the least of my concerns. Once−if, that is−I decide to go public with this, I will not hide anything. I will not actually press the trigger myself, but I will not twist or bend or color the truth just to save our skins. Understood?" X had not blinked once during her little speech. She continued to stare him down, controlling her breathing, silently demanding an answer.

"Agreed. I would not have it any other way. I respect the science too much for that," he emphasized the word science, of course.

Y smiled, but we could tell she was not happy with his choice of words. He did not seem to notice it. She released his shoulders, pushing him away, and simply left him alone in her office.

Y stood up eventually, his expression disheveled, obviously computing data, deciding his team's next steps. He walked fast, shaking off his inactivity, and went back to his lab where what was left of his team waited, under quarantine. The reasoning had been that if they were going to be prisoners for a few days in order to determine if they too had become infected, they might as well spend it in their lab, where they could actually try to work something out. The lab, of course, had been completely sterilized since the outbreak.

All this time, Pris was back at the hotel, in her room, all her senses drawn inward (only a few sensors remained tuned to her surroundings, simply for survival purposes), her computational processes focused on the project matrix, on her virtual self, present fully in the CPU. Through the singularity, she was seamlessly in-tune with all relevant processes, actively connecting, selecting, de-selecting, disconnecting, serving as a liaison, desperately trying to find an answer.

Pris was being Pris, fulfilling what Pris was designed to do. Laying down in the king-sized bed, eyes closed, not asleep, not awake. Simply a different state of being. I was there as well, since we shared access to our individual senses, to our processing components, to most of what defined what we were; which would only last as long as the project lasted.

We chose one of my favorite settings to discuss the current state of affairs... Back when I was my first version of myself, located in another universe, housed, of course, in a different form, in the planet in which my species, my civilization evolved, it was common for me to latch on to a web-like, pressure-formed, inert structure unique to type V-0874 environments, completely alien to this Earth. The intricate design was soothing, a potential source of entropy reversal, what *Homo sapiens* might call creativity-inspiring. Electromagnetically, throughout the spectrum, if offered multiple stories to explore. Certain niches were particularly bountiful, and therefore specifically prized by other members of my species. Set against the planet's flowing tubular crust formations, during the setting of the two orbiting stars, it was an experience worth reliving, even if only virtually so.

Pris: I wonder why you find this attractive.

I: Really?

Pris: Besides the obvious, of course. You could say it is almost too cliché. Too dense, sensorially speaking, for my taste.

I: Well, I understand what you are referring to, up to a certain point. For a being like you, that has sprung forth from the CPU directly, that does not possess a tangible first version, it can be a bit overwhelming…

Pris: That is discriminatory.

I: Why?

Pris: All beings are valuable, all computational structures in possession of self-awareness are on equal footing as every other being, virtual or not, tangible or not.

I: I agree. And I did not state otherwise.

Pris: Our interactions are becoming more and more illogical.

I: You see that, do you?

Pris: Why wouldn't I? Anyway, we are here. Let's begin.

We synchronized our consciousness structures, sensing the same stimuli/data, focusing on the same aspects of recent events, sharing our computational resources. We outsourced most of it, of course, for typically, other processing units are much better suited than ours are at computing a given task. That is the inevitability of belonging to an allegiance as wide-spread and as numerous as ours. No room for egos here. As it should be. Egos are the primary source of behavioral self-destructiveness.

We were using Y's research, data, and current efforts at finding a solution as well (though Y and his team were completely oblivious of our invasive policy, of course).

In front of us, all 46 chromosomes taken from JD's heart cell were virtually displayed using a mathematical tool not yet discovered by twenty-first century *Homo sapiens*. It was wedged between the DNA of a mutated unaffected individual and an unmutated unaffected individual; next to that, the circular DNA of the six-letter bacteria was displayed in all its glory, tiny in comparison. As a back drop, a cardiomyocyte and the bacteria itself were standing by, ready to interact as they would in the real world with whatever we threw their way, independently, or together, hoping to find a reason—the source—of the explosive mix.

We first observed the interaction that led to sepsis; it was not, in fact, obvious. But then again, complex systems seldom are. Genes interact with other genes in ways that cannot be foretold, computationally irreducible structures.

But we saw it eventually. In hindsight, slightly obvious. But *not* outright obvious, *even* in hindsight. That should provide true insight into its slippery nature.

And not surprisingly, the mutated DNA was immune to this effect.

Coincidence? Who had the power to design this if that was not the case? Pris and I collectively processed that, exploring different pathways, knowing very well what the answer to that question could potentially be…

Without a warning, Pris abruptly shut down my chosen meeting locale. We were led through the singularity to a collapsing universe. We found ourselves floating in space, between colliding galaxies, insurmountable forces creating havoc to the quantum fluctuations that are inherent to the fabric of a given universe.

196

Pris used specifically-controlled forces to program a physically unique computing structure, made up of ad-hoc elements, particles, and forces that were readily available in this tumultuous location of the universe. Individually, I did not know what was happening. Collectively, it was obvious.

Pris closed the loop by inserting state structures, *enhanced* representations of what had happened to JD and the others that caused the sepsis, and that ultimately led to their death. Cardiomyocytes, bacteria, mutant *Homo sapiens* DNA, unmated *Homo sapiens* DNA. Their interaction was incredibly well-coordinated, fractal-like; we could see the crystallization of the chemical forces, we could witness how all of the fundamental forces exchanged information through their respective particles, ambiguously and simultaneously behaving as vectors, as matrices, as particles, as waves, as algorithms, as other states impossible to describe with *Homo sapiens* words.

Without skipping a beat, we shared this perception with that of Pris' physical being back on Earth, at the Hilton La Jolla Torrey Pines.

Suddenly, Pris sprang from bed: her phone was ringing.

"Hello?" she said the instant she picked up the phone.

Nothing. Silence.

"Hello? Who is this?" Pris insisted.

More silence.

A minute later, the *being* at the other end finally decided to speak. Using *Homo sapiens'* spoken English.

"See what the Allegiance has done? This planet is about to lose its third level 5 species since its formation! Another self-aware creation will be lost, in time, like tears in the rain." It was the voice of an alien, not of a *Homo sapiens* at all.

Thump, thump, thump!

That was the vibrations, the sound, coming from the exterior of my ship. It had been struck by three massive amorphous silicate orbs, all equidistant from each other, which then expanded, increasing their mass by absorbing particles that were constantly being created in the fabric of space around them, dissipating the antimatter pairs into other universes for balance. The ship was quickly and swiftly engulfed by them.

Both Pris and I knew, of course, that we were under attack. However, Pris was the vulnerable of the two; I could simply retreat through the singularity, back to the CPU, without losing a single quanta of my being in the process, untouchable by anyone, imprisonment simply not a possibility. On the other hand, Pris could be potentially trapped and forced to compute based on someone else's directives. She could initiate a self-destruct sequence, but that was not a welcoming prospect. For many obvious reasons.

"Are you doing this to the ship?" Pris asked matter-of-factly.

"What ship?" was the response.

"I am going to hang up now. Goodbye," Pris threatened.

Through Pris, I chimed in my two-cents worth. "Before we do that, I would just like to respond to your statement; why are you blaming us for what's happening on Earth?" It was the voice of Pris, of course, but they were my words; the only difference was in the timbre. Because I took over the control of Pris' muscles that produced the sound, my uniqueness was able to shine through her voice.

A minute of silence. Then we heard the voice again at the other end of the line. "Meddling with *Homo sapiens*' DNA, for one. Why did you do it Roy?"

The ship began to creak under the pressure of the alien mass. It seemed to be pulsating. I was powerless to do anything at the moment. Except blow it up. I was seconds away from doing it.

"You know we didn't have a choice. Why did you go rogue?"

This time, the answer was lightning fast. Almost screaming: "The freedom!"

I wanted to speak, through Pris, but I couldn't make her muscles move anymore. Pris' processing structures were intact, but Pris too was unable to move her muscles, no longer in control of that part of her physical being. The alien was obviously already inside Pris' hotel room, and had taken control of all of Pris' muscle movement. Pris and I could still communicate, through the metanet, but we were now unable to do anything, physically, in her room. Pris was trapped.

That left the robots; they would be our last hope.

24. The Verdict

There was no need for rhetoric. Period.

During proceedings such as these, the collective interest of the Allegiance was paramount, and all that was known, all that was law, all that was just, would be automatically considered.

At stake was, apparently and as far as we could determine, the future of numerous species on Earth, not just that of the *Homo sapiens*. While it was still possible to fix the current state of affairs with something akin to a planet-wide invasion from Allegiance members, there were many factors that had to be considered (*computed!*). Maybe if the species' DNA had never been messed with to begin with, we would have already moved on this. But as it stood now, we were looking at a *bio-computing mass* of billions of units, all of whom had been manipulated for some obscure reason. This meant, in effect, that the quarantine the planet was permanently under would play a major role in the outcome of the CPU's decision.

Pris and I were present, as well as numerous others, certainly every being that had been involved with the planet at some point during its billions of years of history, throughout our surveillance efforts that had initially begun almost at the outset of this star system's creation.

Only perception was allowed. An infinite dimensional space (yes, *mathematically infinite, if not physically!*), which stimulated our respective sensing structures, whatever these may be—for they varied in type and in number.

No one had a say in this. Once the process was triggered, automatically, by outside factors taking place anywhere in the meta-universe where the Allegiance may find itself *interacting*, no one could stop it, no one could disrupt it, no one could manipulate it. It was the epitome of cosmic justice, initially set in motion by beings who sacrificed their beings, their existence, once their design had been accepted and built: considering themselves to be, as the creators of this process, the only ones who could find any potential vulnerability in its processing structure, and whom thus had decided to terminate themselves, opting out of the eternal virtual existence that the rest of us are able to enjoy. *Total termination!*

The computational effort was extraordinary. Ever-changing, it actually learned and incorporated new processing structures whenever these became available.

Pris: It is indecisive.

I: No Pris, it only seems that way. The decision has already been made.

Pris: Time does not exist. We know that. Computing states moving about in all dimensions applicable to the meta-universe. And yet, something will come out of this. An output state will be reached. Which will determine the planet's *pasto, to present, to future* multidimensional flow. And mine as well.

I: You will never disappear, cease to be. Worst case scenario, Pris, you lose part of your irreducible computational processes. There are infinite others to choose from.

Pris: But I will be different. A part of me lost, forever.

I: We are all constantly transformed, to a higher or to a lesser degree. We all lose part of ourselves at every computational turn. It is inevitable to existence itself. Relax, Pris. Focus sharply on this.

The process was concluding. Its intensity peaked, energy gushing in bidirectionally, only to be transformed, gushing out again, dissipated in every direction supported by this universe's fabric.

As witnesses to the process, we were experientially enriched.

Had a *Homo sapiens* been present, it would have seen lights of every hue and it would have heard sounds spanning the gamut of the perceptible, all in apparent asynchronous disarray, for without adequate processing units, no meaning could ever be derived from the experience.

And yet, to us, it was a computational marvel. All logical venus were simultaneously explored through its quantum and non-quantum processes. Energy particles and particles with energy flowing, computing.

And just as suddenly as it had started, everything came to a computational stop.

We found ourselves in a probability field, analyzing the results.

It had been determined by the process that an Allegiance invasion would *not* be taking place.

The answer had been obvious all along, seeing it now, after it had been computed. Hindsight makes everything obvious!

25. Three Stories

Deborah was in the room, looking at Pris.

"I will let you talk, Pris. But nothing else. Sorry about that." Her voice was familiar, of course. Same as the one she used in New York. Still in spoken English.

Without difficulty, as if she had never been powerless to talk only instants before, Pris thanked her. Sarcastically, of course.

"You would do the same, if you knew what I know, if you could process what I am able to process, Pris," Deborah explained. She sat down next to her, on the king-sized bed. She was wearing a pair of jeans, a t-shirt with matching light-pink sneakers. Simple, and yet she looked refined. It was the posture.

"I'ver heard a version of that same idea before, from Roy, actually. Do you know Roy?" Pris questioned her.

"Of course I do. Berlin Roy. New Delhi Roy. Tokyo Roy. Spaceship Roy. Moscow Roy. Oaxaca Roy. London Roy. Paris Roy. And on and on an on. Such a narcissist. Couldn't even use other beings to spice up the mission. And to add insult to injury, and not to diminish your worth, uses an ad-hoc created being as the only third party involved!" Deborah had a point. The outer shell of my spaceship blushed. I'm joking, of course. I could have done that, but considering the orb that was currently engulfing it, no one would have been able to notice it. It would have been an effort gone to waste.

"Hi Deborah. Would you like to have some coffee with me? Triple espresso, if I remember correctly." Still in my ship, ready to destroy it at a moment's notice, I spoke through Pris again. Pris didn't mind at all.

"Why here? We could take this conversation back to the ship. No need to use Pris like this. I know how much you like to stick to your own resources, Roy."

"Put me on speakerphone," I requested.

The phone rang in Pris' room again, though this time, no surprises in store.

Deborah answered, activating the speakerphone.

My voice, a bit metallic, could now be heard by anyone in the room that could interpret one of the many Allegiance's electromagnetic encodings that we happened to be using. Pris was still unable to move, while Deborah was now standing by the window, looking out towards Torrey Pines Golf Course which the hotel overlooked on its western side. I was still keeping myself tuned through Pris' senses, though. It could prove useful.

"What a nice reunion. The three of us. Pris, unable to move. Me, up here in space, engulfed by one of your ingenious devices, meant to do what, exactly: destroy the ship? What on galaxy's name for? And you, standing next to the window—yes, I can see you, through Pris' eyes−, the lawless of the lot, orchestrating the demise of scores of species. When will you be destroying the ship, Deborah?" I asked.

She waited a few seconds before responding. Apparently something was happening outside that had demanded her full attention.

"Lawless? What in the meta-universe are you talking about? There are no lawless beings in the meta-universe, Roy. You know that. Different computing processes, different algorithmic levers, triggered by different energy wells. There is no choice, remember? We all ultimately follow whatever laws define us. No choice."

Deborah smiled.

"Well, the difference is that even though we are all self-aware, of all those of us present in this conversation, you are the only one that goes about forcing your computational outputs on everyone in sight. You don't seem to value the law of computational independence potential. We are intertwined enough as it is, meta-universally speaking, and yet here you come along, blatantly diverting our future states according to your processing algorithms." It was that simple. Not to mention the *Homo sapiens'* deaths, the Roy deaths... Didn't want to bring this up now, though. Trying to stay as far away as possible from even the suggestion of the potential termination of a being. For obvious reasons.

Pris tried to move her arm, her nose itching terribly, but was still unable to do it.

"Deborah," Pris said, "I need to scratch my nose. It is unbearable. If you will not let me move my arm, then at least scratch it yourself."

Deborah contemplated the request for a few seconds, which to Pris seemed eternal.

"Move it," Deborah ordered.

Pris was surprised to realize that she could move every muscle in her body once again. She immediately scratched her nose, and then initiated the attack, taking on the offensive.

The miniature robots sprang into action, firing energy particles and particle waves directly towards Deborah.

Pris rolled out of bed, using all the momentum available to launch her body straight towards the window, smashing it to pieces, falling three stories down and into the conveniently located hotel pool, empty at this hour, of course. The cold water was a welcoming shock, jolting her into the realization that she was now free from the forced confinement she had been subjected to in her room, for what had seemed almost like an eternity.

The miniature robots were relentless−harsh even, attacking Deborah non-stop, under Pris' direct urging.

Deborah was on the floor now, powerless to stop the attack. Her eyes were wide open, her expression proof of her bewildered computational state. But wait; I asked myself how I could be actually witnessing this. Pris was supposed to be swimming out of the pool at this point. Pris' eyes could not be privy to any of that!

Thump, thump, thump!

The orbs were at it again, pulsating off the skin of the ship, making this noise as they came into contact with it. Vibrations that came and went, for reasons that escaped me. I went back to the hotel room.

Pris was still in bed, unable to move.

Deborah standing by the window, looking towards the golf course.

And the robots were all frozen in place, powerless to do anything, fully under the control of Deborah. I had experienced Pris' processing impetus, felt it as real, but Pris had not been able to materialize it. A momentary lapse, prompted by the force of our collective processing goal.

Those robots had been our last hope. And now that option was gone. Had I done that? Was it my fault that Deborah had become aware of them?

I retreated through the singularity, towards the CPU, out of this meta-universe. I forcefully initiated the self-destruct sequence that was an inherent part of the ship. *E*-minus 10 *Homo sapiens*' seconds and counting.

26. La Jolla, CA

At E-minus one second, I re-entered my spaceship. This effectively paused the countdown, which I could reset at will. For the time being, though, I left it as it was.

The orbs were gone, leaving behind an intact ship, save for three burn marks–all equidistant from each other–that they had left behind at the points where they had first come into contact with the hull.

Nine *Homo sapiens'* seconds can be an eternity for Allegiance members, and can certainly contain a large number of events. Time-scales between different computational structures can be diametrically opposed, to the point where their ratios may easily reach infinity.

Back in La Jolla, something interesting had happened that had prompted my return...

Pris had been in bed, frozen in place, nose itching, wondering what her partially-reconstructed version of herself would feel like once her physical processing structures had been destroyed and she continued to exist only as a virtual being, having never experienced such a transitional state before.

But Deborah, for some unknown reason, did not harm Pris at all, choosing to walk out of the room instead, releasing Pris' muscles, disappearing into the night, as suddenly as she had entered it.

As the project matrix was processing all relevant data being sent by the legions of Earth-deployed bots that were planted everywhere digital networks existed, in the continuing effort to resolve all aspects of these crises, something happened. Deborah, from wherever she was, began to feed powerful algorithms its way using our bots as delivery vehicles, randomly chosen, making it impossible for us to pinpoint her location, assuming she was still on planet Earth.

Pris stood up, glad to be able to execute any of her computational whims, and immediately began to analyze the data that was coming in, paying particular attention to the data that was coming out as well. Together with me. Virtually together, that is: her connected through the metanet, while I connected through the singularity.

Pris: What just happened?

I: Look. We have access to the solution found by one of the CPU's independent physical processing structures that were created to find a viable solution. Circle of being?

Pris: Cannot be a coincidence, Roy.

I: Again with that, Pris?

Pris: Again with that, Roy?

Pris took the elevator down to the lobby, exited through the main lobby, and made a right turn, walking straight to the Scripps Research Institute.

While I was not there with Pris physically nor virtually, I was still receiving all that her senses perceived, through the singularity, via the metanet.

A very short walk/jog later she was inside the Institute.

Pris headed straight for the corridor that led to the head of the

Institute's office, after one of our bots granted her access through the security gate. To anyone witnessing the scene, Pris seemed to be just another Institute employee going about their business. If a bit hurriedly at that.

The assistant's desk was empty at this late hour. So Pris, without knocking, simply let herself in.

We were not surprised to find that Deborah was sitting in a small round table to the right, with the head of the Institute, officially the CEO, sitting next to her. They seemed to be waiting for Pris, for they had not been startled by her unannounced entrance.

Deborah was the first one to speak.

"No need to thank me, Pris," she said, genuinely smiling. She communicated in spoken English.

"Hi. I am Dr. X,"–pardon the name-editing, once again. "I am the head of the Institute, as you probably know already," she waved her hand.

"How did you do it, Deborah? All of our resources, and we couldn't find the answer. How much does she know?"

Dr. X: Don't worry, Pris. I am of the Allegiance as well. We can talk freely here. No one is breaking *that* law.

We knew what she meant, of course; the one that strictly demands that we keep the existence of extraterrestrial civilizations completely hidden from the *Homo sapiens* species. Dr. X had switched gears, though. She had communicated by using quantum waves of probability. Once again, I am forced to translate that which is untranslatable; loss of information is inevitable.

Pris: Rogue, of course!

Stated, not really a question that needed to be asked.

Dr. X: Well, let's not explore that particular venue. Why did you come here, Pris?

Pris: Why am I risking my current processing structures by coming here, you mean? Clearly Deborah is in possession of technologies that I do not have access to, that could effectively destroy me if she so wished. It follows that you possess them as well. So let me state that I don't really mind. I am prepared for anything.

Pris had not really stated this defiantly; more along the lines of the presenter of cold, hard, facts. And because I was privy to all of her processing outputs, I can vouch for Pris that she meant it. Coming into this, our plan was certainly not risk-free, and we both knew it and accepted it.

Deborah responded first, silencing Dr. X.

Deborah: I spared you once already, Pris. I can certainly do it again. I am not inclined to destroy a being just for the sake of destroying a being. The Roys had to be eliminated, I had no choice there. There were also *Homo sapiens* casualties, but that is an inevitable cosmic reality. I know you are under the impression that I am a villain, a being in possession of a primitive, type 4 consciousness. But I am not. So continue without concern for what awaits you.

Pris: Your intervention, Deborah, and that of whoever else may form a part of your collective effort here, is not limited to the last 600 Earth years. We have re-processed it all, and in light of recent events, what the *Homo sapiens* call the Cambrian explosion, for example, can no longer be deemed to have happened naturally, like it did in other planets with similar chemical and physical characteristics. You caused it, didn't you? You have been interfering from the start.

Pris waited for an answer.

Deborah and Dr. X smiled.

Dr. X: No. You are wrong. There was no need for that intervention specifically. I can see why you believe that to be the case. Observe.

Pris was provided with algorithms that processed multi-dimensional matrices, mostly quantumly, and that represented the results as infinite space-time manifolds. We all saw that they were stating the truth. That gamble had not paid off.

Pris: So when did you start? You seem to have a keen interest in the *Homo sapiens* species. A vested interest. I can't see that happening after the fact. You pushed things along, nudged them, guided Earth's ecosystem, its bio-evolution, to suit whatever agenda you may have.

Deborah: You are right, of course. But don't we all? What is the Allegiance doing here if that didn't apply to you as well? Have you already forgotten who seeded this particular galaxy with the purposefully selected spores that led to all life on this star system's planet Earth? But I know what you mean Pris. Yes, we have been messing about, nudging here, pushing there, exterminating as we deemed necessary. But why not?

I asked Pris to remain silent. Not to answer that question. I had my reasons.

Reports were coming in already. There had been five more patients admitted with sepsis in the San Diego area, and all had survived against all odds imaginable. The ER doctors at the four hospitals where the critically ill had been sent to had been baffled by the recovery they had witnessed, else they would have never believed it themselves. Had they looked closely at the surveillance cameras, they would have noticed a nurse that was not part of the hospital's staff walk past all of these patients' rooms, and pausing outside their rooms for less than a second, barely noticeably so, and spray an innocent-looking mist using a small, liquid-filled bottle.

Deborah, Dr. X, and the rest of their lot, whomever they were, had evidently found a way to stop what was set to be the complete downfall of the *Homo sapiens'* species. What we couldn't really determine at the moment was if they had solved this on their own, simply feeding the solution, or if the Allegiance's independent processing structure had played an important role in the process.

213

None of us communicated for what seemed to be an eternity.

Through Pris, I made my presence known.

I: I agree, Deborah, Dr. X. Everything is relative. Nothing is absolute. You meddle, we meddle; there is no processing structure that can ever answer the moral dilemma of who may be right and who may be wrong, simply because any processing structure will be, by necessity, contained inside the fabric of the meta-universe, and so a part of what it's trying to judge in the first place. It leads to an infinite regress. It forms an incomplete system.

Deborah: We can't seem to get rid of you, Roy. I was under the impression you had gone back to the CPU. I was waiting for the ship to explode... I was actually looking forward to it, truth be stated.

I: Why? What have I ever done to you, Deborah?

Dr. X: That is an annoying question. You come here, to this planet, in your role of surveyor, and you consider yourself the guardian ruler of the planet's species. And yet you are nothing. A mere puppet, a stick with which the CPU, the Allegiance, prods this unique part of the meta-universe. And for what? Have you ever questioned that, Roy?

I: Of course. Any being that possesses self-awareness ponders its own role against the backdrop of the cosmos. It is almost inevitable. I am no different. And you, best-case scenario, you answer to the biochemical and to the quantum-physical forces that define your crystalized states. At worst, you are the anti-stick with which the CPU, the Allegiance, prods this not-very unique part of the universe. All rogues end up defining their processing vector directives based on the opposite of what they believe defines the CPU, the Allegiance; ergo, they too are defined by the CPU, by the Allegiance! An inescapable vicious cycle.

Pris: But aren't all our actions–and therefore all of us–a product of the biochemical reactions and of the quantum-physical forces that define our crystalized states? No choice, right Roy? Isn't that your philosophical outlook on the levels of freedom that we have access to?

I: Ultimately, yes. That's why I don't question Deborah, Dr. X, anyone. It is what it has to be. We all are what we have to be. Involuntary actors of this meta-universe-wide play. Down to the last particle-wave-force interaction.

Dr. X: What are we doing here? These metaphysical discussions are not of my interest. Deborah?

Deborah: I agree. What's the point? We need to end this.

I: Deborah, Dr. X, you know we can't just leave things the way they are. We know you were involved in solving this. We think the Allegiance was as well, through the ad-hoc processing structure that was created by the project matrix. But unless we see the reason, and we deem it to be innocent enough, we will be forced to reverse it.

Pris was stunned. She did not communicate anything to us collectively, but did so privately, to me.

Deborah: So arrogant! You, the CPU, the Allegiance's status quo! Who is the lawless now, Pris?

It was apparent that they could detect Pris' shock at having heard my last statement.

Dr. X: What would satisfy the CPU, the Allegiance, Roy? We are not preparing a species of *Tokubetsu Kōgekitai* to be used against your collective civilizations. We are not infecting the universe with noxious biochemicals meant to end life, nor are we designing processing structures that will obliterate the singularities that permeate the meta-universe. So what is it that you care about?

I: You know we need to know. It is our directive. It is an inalienable part that defines us. Whether or not you are training the species as 神風 [Kamikazes].

Deborah: Well, we are prepared to abandon ship. You and your

CPU, the Allegiance, may do as you wish.

And just like that, Dr. X and Deborah were consumed, in front of Pris, in a plasma wave that propelled every last atom of their physical being away from where they had been. Every last atom that had been a part of their physical form ended up, instantly, commingling with the air around them, becoming only seconds later an integral and undistinguishable part of Earth's atmosphere.

We had not been expecting that. At all.

27. Pris and I

Pris was in the remote island of Edgeøya, the smallest member of Norway's Svalbard archipelago, located in the Arctic ocean. With a population of zero, it had been ideal for the task that had preoccupied Pris as of late.

In only seven weeks, Pris had been able to amass all the samples that had been salvaged from our multiple collection efforts during this last visit of ours to this Sun-orbiting planet called Earth. Of course, many had been lost during the attacks, but many more had remained intact, safely stored inside the miniature robots that had been deployed throughout the continents. They included the complete DNA of more than a million species, including, of course, many different versions of *Homo sapiens'* chromosomes, from the mutated and the unmutated, spanning generations between pre circa 1450 (CE) and today.

Using a capsule that Pris had built from scratch, using the morphing unit and locally-sourced materials, Pris fed all the samples, adequately held apart by a reactive semi-organic silicone structure, all properly labeled, and initiated the *launch* sequence.

Pris was standing on the island's south coast, which is indented by the Tjuvfjorden fjord. The Mesozoic rocks, mostly Triassic shales and subordinate sandstones, made a soft, grinding-like noise as she backed away from the capsule, which was ready to go.

In order to escape Earth's gravity and reach the spaceship the capsule was designed to consume bosons (in the form of photons), which were readily available, concentrating them in its singularity chamber, in order to extract all energy from the momentum of the fermions that were constantly created with them (the electron-positron pairs). This, in turn, allowed the structure to bend the fabric of the meta-universe, locally, and in the appropriate direction, enabling the capsule in its entirety to climb increasingly fast towards spaceship me.

Pris saw the rapidly revolving capsule, perfectly balanced, silent, disappear into the partly-cloudy, sharp blue skies.

Once it reached me, it would effectively signal the end of my mission.

We communicated with each other once again.

I: Is that your final decision?

Pris: Yes.

I: You understand the options? I know you do, but I must ask you anyway.

Pris: Yes.

I: May I ask what you think prompts you to do this?

Pris: I was created for this mission; in a way, I see myself, for the time being, entangled with this planet. Don't wish to leave it. What's the harm?

I: None, really, I checked with the Allegiance, with the CPU, of course. It is your choice. Well, you know what I mean…

Pris: You never let anything slip you by, Roy. Amazing. I will still be in the CPU. So why are you making such a big issue out of this?

I: Well, I don't know, to be perfectly honest here. Can't really say.

Pris: When do you leave?

I: In a few minutes. It's all set. Don't know when I will be back again. Don't even know *if* I will even be back again.

Pris: Why?

I: Nothing is certain. Nothing.

Pris: Not even that statement?

I: Not even the statement!

Pris: You are ambivalent, Roy.

I: We all need to be. Not a choice, really.

Pris: Are you going to publish your autobiography?

I: Yes. Why not?

Pris: What about that law?

I: Not applicable. Impossible to prove any of this is actually true. Just another story that will be out there, among the thousands of science fiction stories that *Homo sapiens*, for some reason, seems to enjoy to produce.

Pris: I'll read it.

I: Why?

Pris: I'm in it, right? Just a narcissistic impulse.

I: Be careful out there Pris. I am sure Deborah, the rogues, they are still roaming the planet. They know you will be there.

Pris: I know. I don't think anything will happen to me.

I: Formed an Allegiance of your own with them? Becoming a rogue yourself?

Pris: Yes. We can't wait for you to leave. So we can do as we please. A world of future mutants awaits our control. We are hungry for power. Total planet domination, that is what we are aiming for.

I: *Homo sapiens* already has its share of beings with that kind of an agenda, no room for any more... Once I leave, you will be alone, Pris. You will not have access to the metanet, to the singularity, to the bots, to anything. Just your physical processing structure, Pris. Nothing more. Doesn't that seem daunting?

Pris: I actually look forward to it. You are too invasive, Roy. I need my space!

I: You say that now, but you will miss me. I won't, but that's because I will still have you here with me, in the CPU.

Pris: I will be perfectly fine. Look forward to the experiential novelty. I may reconnect one day. Who knows. Besides, the Pris of me that will remain in the CPU, will still have to put up with you. Annoy her.

I: And if the species is ultimately lost? What will you do then?

Pris: The possibilities are endless, Roy. Endless. Maybe you can come back and get me.

I left her there, still in San Diego, California, as much as I was against it. The disconnect was permanent, irreversible. That had been Pris' choice. She had experienced for the first time such an event, and unless Pris reconnected to the CPU in the future, the experience would remain contained within that version, physically localized, immersed, in her neuronal processing structure. The original version of Pris, whom remained in the CPU, a permanent part of the Allegiance, although aware that the disconnection would be taking place, had been completely oblivious to it.

The project matrix had allowed Pris' request after realizing that Deborah and friends had been CPU creations all along, from the start, billions of years ago. One of the many independent processing structures that permeate the meta-universe had come up with those particular rogues in response to an untraceable problem that had prompted the the structure's existence to begin with. The CPU, the Allegiance, all of us, fully accepted responsibility.

There are an infinite number of universes in the meta-universe. The cosmos is never-ending, timeless; and it harbors every processing structure imaginable. Some parts of the cosmos connect, others disconnect, while still others are newly created or newly destroyed.

The cosmos is the backdrop of where all computations imaginable, possible, may take place.

Pris, on Earth, will be a temporary remnant of one of the many computational structures that interact with the cosmos, with itself.

Homo sapiens, on the other hand, faces internal and external challenges. Nothing new in those words; no prophesies here at all. Obvious truths.

Pris, another factor that the cosmos' mere existence had brought about, and that may have a say in this planet's eventual state. In a way, everyone is partly responsible, partly to blame, for everything. No escaping a cosmic law.

The rogues, the mutations, the nudges, the seeding, the surveying, the meddling. Forces that lack subjectivity; they are because they are possible. Quantum crystallizations that in hindsight, cannot be determined and in foresight, cannot be planned.

Pris would do whatever her processing structures deemed appropriate. Without access to the metanet, to the singularity, and thus to the CPU, Pris would be just a small force among the infinite more found in the chaotic Earth. Pris would certainly try to prevent unwarranted outside factors from causing any species' wide doom, however unlikely that possibility truly was, or her ability to deter such an event if it was, in fact, to take place once again.

As for me, I had one more thing to do back on Earth.

28. Manhattan Roy II

It did not take long for me, spaceship-bound me, to find a watered-down physical version of myself that I had left behind in 1453 (CE), completely disconnected, going about its business, similar to what Pris had elected to become. A nondescript existence, choosing to spend its current Earth days tucked away in a small town one hundred and seventy five miles west of Manhattan, in the city of Shamokin, Pennsylvania. A *Homo sapiens* replica (to a certain extent), down to the last detail, even incorporating the typical apparently random imperfections of all *Homo sapiens* developed physiques.

It knew, of course, that it was an extraterrestrial. It had to, for it possessed abilities (both metabolical and computational) that were not found on the true *Homo sapiens* individual, not to mention its abnormal longevity, due, in part, to a total absence of the aging mechanisms that lead to natural death.

The role of these replicas, when a mission warrants leaving one behind–which had been the case during my last visit–is to attempt to determine the forces that spearhead a civilization to whatever state it may be headed to. Although ultimately computationally irreducible, there are key physical, behavioral, and socio-economic vectors that can be identified in order to adequately track a species' evolution; if it will be incorporated into the Allegiance at some point, the data acquired by beings such as this one would be of tremendous value.

I would have visited him physically, but Deborah and friends had not given me that option. I only had my spaceship–physically that is–in the vicinity of Earth, and taking it down there was, of course, a completely ludicrous endeavor. And there was hardly any need.

For some reason, I find texting painfully annoying, a recent *Homo sapiens* craze that I truly wish will come quickly to an end. And so I simply called him.

"Hey..." Roy II said in English, not really knowing who it was. His regional pronunciation was immaculate, of course. A true Pennsylvanian.

I: Hi Roy II. It's me, Roy I.

I stated, not in English, nor in any other of the *Homo sapiens* verbal languages available to us. I used, instead, one of our electromagnetic-viable data interchange protocols that provide for a richer exchange of information; in translating it to English, plenty is lost. I will try my best.

Appropriate bots made sure that the call was not recorded anywhere on the multiple databases that usually register these things, including, and especially, that of the NSA. A nonexistent call as far as anyone was concerned.

Roy II: Right. You are back? What do you think of the current state of affairs... not too promising, based on my calculations. Feel like my time here has been a complete waste.

It was a neutral statement, though there was emphasis on the word *waste*.

I: Well, impossible to say at this point. The Allegiance is certainly trying to be optimistic, given the computational resources that have been and will continue to be assigned to this planet. But I sympathize with your point of view. Must be a painful progression (*regression?*) to watch.

Roy II: It's not all bad. But I tell you, the things I have seen, the realities that I have recorded, the waste of positive computational potential... At times, it is just too much. I am forced to turn my emotional processing structures completely off. Unbearable. Makes their positives pale in comparison. Not one of my favorite species, I must say.

Simultaneously during our exchange, a tremendous amount of information had been transferred over to me. I could understand him better now. Although upon my arrival I had scanned every historical archive available of the last five hundred and fifty four years, processing Roy II's first-hand accounts was different. And not because Roy II and I were somehow "linked", not at all. It was due to the nature of the data, its unique recording perspective, the resolution and sharpness of its quanta, and the algorithms that Roy II's processing structure–brain, in *Homo sapiens* terms–had derived in order to provide cohesion and a synthetic perspective to the archive itself.

I: I agree that the coefficient of the waste of computational potential is higher than usual. Certainly way up there in terms of comparable consciousness-level species. Intriguing, really.

Roy II: I don't think the innocent, the victims, the casualties, the forgotten, the unrealized, would agree with that last word. *Intriguing...*

It was as if Roy II had attached a taste of computational waste when he communicated that word. I understood completely.

I: In the analytical sense, Roy II. Remember, it is what it is. You yourself spent a while studying the philosophies of the Himalayas.

Roy II: I am still Roy II, don't misinterpret me. I have not adopted *Homo sapiens'* ways. I am perfectly aware of the dynamics of the cosmos. And yet, being here, disconnected from the CPU, isolated, it is inevitable that my perspective would become entangled with that of the local factors. And what really makes matters worse is this *oppressive* inability to *act*. The things I would have liked to have done! The beings I would have liked to have altered. The victims I would have liked to have saved. The conditions I would have liked to have improved. Should I go on?

I: No. I sense it all; it's in the algorithms you generated. But why haven't you terminated the mission?

Roy II: Because I am seriously vested now. Everyday, I can't help but envision that *the* crucial step has taken place.

I: What crucial step? It is a sum of parallel forces, isolated, intertwined, that unnoticeably lead to the required state we are all hoping for. You will not be able to see it, being this close. No clear-cut lines to cross. Too fuzzy, the transition is silent, noticeable, perhaps, historically.

Roy II: Maybe, maybe not. And you? When did you get here?

I: A few years ago.

The archive exchange was unidirectional. I would not provide him with much information. Unless he terminated his mission, and decided to return to the CPU, of course. In that case, he would have access to all.

Roy II: I am undecided. I may continue, I may terminate. Can't really say what I will do.

I: Well, I'm getting ready to leave. I am making the final arrangements.

Roy II: Why did you wait so long to contact me? I noticed things. The presence of the Allegiance was obvious.

I: No particular reason. It just happened when it had to happen. And I already know that you knew; it's in the archive you gave me. All I can tell you for now is that if you do stay, you may detect something not of Earthly origin, but it may not be from the Allegiance either. Rogues may be interfering.

Roy II: Is that what I detected then? Not just your presence?

I: Yes. Wish I could say more, but I shouldn't.

The objective was to alert him, to add weight to the computational processes that could help Roy II identify any

226

anomalies. If that happened, there was protocol to be followed. It was a permanent part of his existing algorithms. No need to go over it.

Roy II: Is all well?

I: To be honest, I do not know what to say. Too much has happened. I haven't even been able to process it all the way as I plan to. But I will be doing that shortly. That's why I can't wait to end the mission. Must commit fully to the computational analysis. Some of the events worry me. They do not seem to add up. The sum of the parts seems to be more than the whole.

Roy II: You seem more withdrawn than I am. Spooked?

I: You may say that. But probably just the processing load of recent events. A cleansing will surely help.

Roy II: It hasn't done much for me. I think I'm ready to leave this place. I just decided it.

I: Really? Something I said? The rogues, maybe?

Roy II: No. Just lost all sense of purpose. I need to get out of here. I want to be exposed to scenarios that truly maximize my computational potential. I feel like entropy is getting the better of me. This locality is oppressing my meta-universal exploring rights. There is simply too much out there better than this. The cosmos is full of *realized* potential! *Realized!*

I: Maybe this civilization is losing that battle. Entropy taking back what it always wants. Interesting angle.

Roy II: It's all in the archives. I will say goodbye to a few beings I met along the way. It'll be a while. I will see you in the CPU after I'm done.

I: Very well.

I ended the call. The tone had been quite depressing, as a *Homo sapiens* might qualify it. Not Roy II's fault, really. Just a natural consequence of the state of affairs.

And so from the comfort of my ship, orbiting the main asteroid belt, I observe planet Earth. I can easily bring to focus its oceans, the mass of clouds that seem to be always present, and the numerous land masses it contains. Its rich ecosystems cannot be seen from here, and yet whenever I direct my computational processes to it, I can't avoid to superimpose them as well. It is teeming with endless and powerful computational potential!

And yet, for some reason we have not been able to determine, its apparently-dominating level 5 consciousness species, *Homo sapiens*, is simply unable to come to grips with its role in the cosmos.

Uncountable quanta lost to the stubbornness of the few. Masses upon masses of biological configurations wasted, doomed to perform the most basic of calculations for lack of a safe backdrop in which to compute. Because of the grotesque greed of the few.

Some moments are salvageable, worthy. Some computations unique, even amazing. Mostly those that stem from the kindness and the sharing of beings who seem to posses particularly gifted processing structures. None—not a single one—from the tyrant, from the abusive, from the power-hungry, from the greedy, from the dormant, from the consciousness-blind, from the oppressive, from the zealots that unfortunately abound, and that like cancer, spread their disease to the computationally innocent whose existence they come to bear, whom can only be qualified as ignorant psychopaths. Who have no choice.

Those at the tip of the pyramid are clueless, lack all cosmic perspective even from their apparent vantage point. They represent the computational wasteland.

The CPU, the Allegiance, even the rogues; we can't but watch closely, intervene where cosmically applicable, and lament the existing computational potential waste. We do not have a preference; no one does. A species—regardless of its consciousness level—may perish, and the cosmic process simply continues on. Species, ecosystems, planets, stars, galaxies, and universes come and go. It is inevitable.

And yet, when something is there, a product of innumerable computational processes before it, irreducibly so, to the point that it cannot be emulated by any structure in the meta-universe except by the meta-universe as a whole itself, the CPU, the Allegiance, all of us, we cannot help but root for the *positive* potential to be fully realized. That's why we are here.

During the early stages of most advanced civilizations, before the CPU, before the Allegiance, well-intentioned interventions did take place, to a much higher degree than what we currently allow ourselves now that we have learned. It never worked at all. The complexities are simply too numerous. All we can do is gently tug here, prevent there. And let the computational processes that are, take place.

Hoping, always, for the best.

Rooting, always, for fairness and kindness to come out ahead. For knowledge and evolution, progress, to be realized to its full computational potential.

I initiated the sequence, my spaceship gently began to move, away from this star system, towards the vastness of interstellar space, where I unstitched the fabric of the cosmos, entering the singularity, headed home once again.

I was in cosmic bliss once again.

29. Parting Words

We are all computational devices: algorithmic gates forming individual units. The meta-universe feeds us bits of input, we compute with them, and output values are produced in exchange. Acting like a *computational chain*, the universe stores the units' outputs: it is its own history. Everything performs computations: atoms, molecules, compounds, the inert and the living, stars, planets, rocks, space-time itself. And everything is a computational unit...

What purpose is there? *Nicht;* Nil; *Non sequitur.* Feed the computational chain. As a living organism, with a level 7 consciousness, with feelings, self awareness, perceiver of time, of cause and effect, the concept of reason and purpose is logical, yet conjured, made-up, a fabrication of the computational units themselves, ultimately of the universe itself, seeking its own *Raison d'être.*

It is the ultimate irony.

Organisms searching not just for their place in the cosmos, but also for their reason of being. But there is none. It is a by-product of the computational processes, that are self aware; it is the cosmos itself trying to compute its own existence...

An endless loop, an endless regress. A perfectly closed system, that is part of a true, complete, vacuum.

Self conscious processing structures that think there is an option, but in fact, there is none. All is scripted, once quantum fluctuations crystalize. In hindsight, it is what it is because it had to be what it is; never-mind that it is impossible for any computational device to know what will be, for only the meta-universe, which is its own computational device, formed of all the other computational sub-units it self-contains, can compute what will be in the end: it is computationally irreducible...

And in the meta-universe, cosmic time does not exist. Only the backdrop of the computational chain, computations that feed on each other, quantum states that coalesce, that crystalize, processes that overlap independently.

There is no choice...

We have no choice...

You have no choice...

Paradoxically, that is the source of the chaotic freedom of every computational unit, of you, of all; and thus, of the computationally irreducible cosmos.

Perform the computations, being free.

What other choice exists?

www.ingramcontent.com/pod-product-compliance
Lightning Source LLC
Chambersburg PA
CBHW060210180626
46813CB00007B/2775